New York Times and *USA Today* Bestselling Author

CYNTHIA
EDEN

Forbidden
BITE

This book is a work of fiction. Any similarities to real people, places, or events are not intentional and are purely the result of coincidence. The characters, places, and events in this story are fictional.

Published by Hocus Pocus Publishing, Inc.

Proof-reading by: J. R. T. Editing

PROLOGUE

"Don't look into her eyes. If you do, she'll take your soul."

Griffin Romeo tried really, really hard not to laugh in the face of his newest client. "No eyes," he murmured. "Check."

Felix Flemming slammed his clenched fist onto the top of Griffin's desk. "Listen to me! *Listen to me!* This shit is for real. You're going to think that she looks innocent. You're going to think that she's the sexiest thing you've ever seen. You're going to think the woman is a walking wet dream—"

"I get it," Griffin interrupted with a sigh. "The lady I'm after is hot, but trust me, I'm a professional. I'm hardly the type to be taken in by a pretty face." What did he look like? An amateur? He'd been in the PI business for five years. He was the best of the fucking best.

"She's killed, man." Felix ran a shaking hand over his face. "She's so small, I don't even know how she does it. This woman is taking out men twice her size. She kills them. She cuts their throats. And Isabella laughs while they bleed."

"And you've seen her do this?" Griffin knew he had to be very careful with the questions that he asked.

"*Yes.* I've seen her shove a man—a guy who had to weigh over 200 pounds—against a dirty alley wall. She threw him like he was *nothing.* Then she went for his throat, and I saw the blood on her." He gave a hard nod. "Yeah, I've witnessed her attack with my own eyes."

"Then why haven't you gone to the cops?" Griffin drummed his fingertips against the armrest on his desk chair. He made sure to let no expression cross his face.

"I've tried! They didn't believe me. I even took them to the scene—to the exact spot where I saw her attack that poor man! But he wasn't there. *She* wasn't there. And Isabella had cleaned up the blood."

Isabella. Isabella Abandonato.

She was to be his new prey.

"I want you to follow her. I want you to track every single move that she makes. Catch her in the act." Felix was sweating. Behind the lenses of his glasses, his bright blue eyes gleamed with intensity.

Griffin gave a low whistle. "Normally, when my clients want me to catch someone in the act...They're talking about a different act." Sex, not murder.

Felix's cheeks reddened. "We have to stop her. The woman is an abomination. She's evil.

Isabella is seducing men and then killing them. The cops won't believe me. So you will get me the proof I need. You *have* to get it for me. Follow her. Watch her. Stalk her."

"And when I do catch her in the, uh, act? What happens to the poor fool she's attacking? Do you expect me to just stand there and watch her kill so that you'll have your precious proof?"

"No, of course not!" Felix began to pace the small confines of Griffin's Las Vegas office. "I expect you to stop her before she kills anyone." He waved his hand vaguely toward Griffin. "I assume you carry a weapon. You have skills, right?"

Actually, Griffin didn't carry a weapon. It was his policy to never carry a gun or a knife. He didn't need those things. He had a special way of defending himself. "To be clear, you aren't hiring me to kill this woman, are you?" The question had to be asked.

"I'm hiring you to stop a monster. Get the proof. Then we can go to the cops, and she can be locked away for the rest of her life." The sound of his ragged breathing seemed to fill the room. After a moment, Felix murmured, "That's exactly what Isabella deserves."

"Then by all means, let's give her what she deserves." Griffin let his gaze sweep over Felix's fancy suit and well-polished shoes. Griffin could practically smell the money dripping off the guy. Griffin had a very, very good sense of smell. This fellow was old money, and a lot of it. "For a surveillance case like this one, my rate is five grand a day."

Felix didn't even blink. "Done."

Hell, yes. For that kind of cash, Felix had just gotten himself one top of the line PI. It was time for Griffin to hunt a monster.

"But remember," Felix blurted. "Don't look into her eyes. Because if you do—"

Griffin shrugged away Felix's words. "Yeah, yeah, I got it. Isabella will take my soul."

"You've been warned."

CHAPTER ONE

Isabella Abandonato didn't look like a killer. She was petite, had curves for fucking miles, golden skin—absolutely lickable skin—and hair as black as night. She wore high, spikey, blood-red heels as she strolled down the sidewalk. Her hips moved with a sexy little roll even as her heels tap-tapped against the pavement. She sauntered right past the line of bars, ignoring the catcalls that were sent her way. She never even glanced at the admiring men. Her head was down, and her eyes seemed to be on the sidewalk in front of her.

If she'd bothered to glance around, Isabella might've realized that she had a stalker. Actually, Griffin had been following her for several nights. So far, the dark-haired beauty had shown no sign of any murderous tendencies. Maybe Felix had been wrong about her.

Abruptly, Isabella turned into the narrow alley way to her left.

Griffin's eyes narrowed. For the past three nights, Isabella had taken her time walking around the Vegas streets. Not the main strip, she never went there. Isabella preferred the slightly shadier spots in Sin City. But she hadn't ventured into an alley on his watch, at least, not until now.

A man wearing a battered leather jacket hurriedly followed Isabella into the alley. At the sight of that guy going after her, Griffin tensed. It was never a good sign when a man followed a woman into an alley. Griffin rolled back his shoulders, and he marched determinedly forward. So far, he'd taken a hands-off approach to Isabella's case. He'd been watching her, every night since Felix had hired him, but Griffin hadn't made contact with her. He hadn't gotten touching close. It appeared that situation was about to change.

As he entered the narrow alley way, Griffin heard a short, desperate cry. Basically, it was a choked gasp. As if someone had tried to call out, but the cry was stifled. Griffin immediately went on high alert. He advanced with a lunge and then he saw —

The asshole in the leather jacket had pinned Isabella to one of the damned dirty walls in the alley. The bastard's right hand was curled around her throat, and the guy's left hand gripped a knife. The tip of the knife was pressed to her cheek.

Oh, the hell, no. That jerk was not going to cut her perfect face. Snarling, Griffin raced forward, but before he could grab the bastard with the knife, Isabella attacked.

One moment, she was staring with wide, desperate eyes at her assailant.

And in the next moment, she'd ripped the knife from the guy's fingers. Isabella threw the knife toward a pile of garbage, and she launched her body at the man. They slammed into the pavement, with Isabella landing on top of her attacker. She grabbed his arms and shoved them over the man's head. Then her face — her mouth — flew right toward the guy's throat.

The bastard screamed.

"What in hell…?" Griffin stopped in shock.

At his words, Isabella's head snapped up. Beneath the moonlight, he could see her wide, gleaming gaze. He could see her small, straight nose. He could see her high cheekbones. He could see her full, sexy lips.

And he could see her fangs. Long, razor-sharp, vampire fangs. Bloody vampire fangs because she'd just attacked the dumbass in the leather jacket.

For a moment, Isabella simply stared at Griffin. Then she licked her lips. "Oh, my." Her voice was just as sexy as he'd imagined. Husky, sinful. "This is awkward."

Griffin's hands fisted at his sides. "You have no idea."

The man beneath Isabella let out a pain-filled groan.

Griffin's gaze immediately jerked toward the fellow, and in that instant, Isabella sprang into action. She flew toward Griffin, and her hands wrapped around his shoulders. She pushed back until he hit the side wall of the alley. She held him there, using a fierce strength that shouldn't have been possible given the size of her small body.

But then again, it shouldn't have been possible for her to sprout fangs, either.

He expected her to go straight for his throat. Griffin was prepared for that move. Instead, a faint furrow appeared between her delicate brows.

"You were trying to help me, weren't you? That's why you came rushing up. You were— *are*—a...Good Samaritan?" Her voice rose faintly with that question.

Yeah, sure, they can go with that label. Griffin considered his options.

Her voice became even breathier as Isabella suddenly pleaded, "Will you please walk out of this alley and forget that you ever saw me? Could you do me that favor? *Please?*"

Forgetting her would be absolutely impossible. Lying? Absolutely doable. "I've already forgotten." His voice had come out rough, with a growling edge.

Instead of appearing reassured by his words, her eyes narrowed. "Who are you?" Her hands still gripped his shoulders, and the sharp edges of her fangs peeked out behind her lips.

I'm the man who was hired to hunt you. Hunt her and…stop her. Fucking hell, Felix had been right about her all along.

Once more, the man on the ground groaned. Griffin wondered…was she going to finish off that fellow? Was Isabella going to drain him dry and leave the guy's dead body in the alley?

"Who. Are. You?" Now, impatience thickened her voice.

Immediately, his gaze snapped back to hers. And that was when he remembered Felix's warning. *Don't look into her eyes.*

Her eyes took on a faint glow. "You will tell me who you are."

"Griffin. Griffin Romeo."

"Griffin." She seemed to taste the name. "Now tell me why you came into this alley."

"Following you." A fast, hard response.

Her head tilted a bit as she studied him. Isabella still didn't ease her grip on his shoulders. He dwarfed her in size. Griffin was well over six feet, and Isabella probably clocked in at around five feet. But her strength…

Supernatural.

She's a vampire. I'm staring at a vampire.

"Following me," she repeated. "To…save me?"

"Knew he was bad news…never follow a woman into an alley for a good…reason." Griffin's words were gritted from between clenched teeth.

"I guess not. But then, that was my plan. To find someone who wasn't exactly...good." Her gaze fell from his. "I feel less guilty that way. It's bad enough that I have to take the blood, but hurting someone—" She broke off. "Forget it." Her eyes rose to meet his once more. "Actually, forget everything." Her order seemed to ring with power. "Forget the alley, forget me. Definitely forget the blood. Walk out of here and go be a Good Samaritan somewhere else." And with that, she let him go.

Isabella turned her back on him and moved to stand over her leather jacket clad prey.

Griffin exhaled slowly. There had been a whole lot of power in her voice. And in her eyes. *Don't look into her eyes.* Felix had been right on that count, but Griffin was betting the guy didn't truly understand just what Isabella was.

I understand plenty.

She'd used a compulsion on him. Because of what she'd done to him, he should walk right out of that alley and never look back. Griffin took one step forward. Then another.

Isabella had knelt next to her prey.

Was she preparing for another bite?

Griffin was right beside her. She was still not even looking at him, so confident of her power...

Too confident.

He grabbed her. In one move, Griffin yanked Isabella off the cracked and stained pavement and up into his arms. He'd whirled her to face him, and he'd pulled out the weapon he'd made sure to pack earlier, just in case. Griffin shoved that weapon right against her chest.

"What are you doing—" Isabella began angrily, but then she stopped, her eyes widening, as she glanced down at her chest.

"Yeah, sweetheart, it's a wooden stake. And, in case the question is coming, if I shove the stake into your heart, no, you *wouldn't* be the first vamp I've killed."

She trembled against him.

"So how about you don't try your mind games anymore? 'Cause, newsflash, they don't work on me."

A tear leaked from her eye. An actual fucking tear. That was new. He'd never seen a vamp cry before. Usually, they were too busy attacking humans—or becoming pure dust after they'd been staked.

"Who are you?" she whispered.

"Already told you that. Griffin Romeo."

"*What* are you?"

"Ah, now, sweetheart, that is a very good question." He smiled at her, and Griffin deliberately let his own fangs flash.

Her mouth parted in surprise.

He gave a mocking laugh. "What? Did you think vamps were the only ones with bite in this town?" Not even close.

"L-let me go." She actually sounded afraid. Total bullshit. She was just trying to scam him. As if he'd be dumb enough to buy a vamp's fear.

"Not happening. You and I—we're heading out of this alley. You'll stay by my side every moment until we get to my ride. You so much as twitch funny, and this stake will sink into your heart."

She just stared at him. He could see the darkness of her eyes—big, deep, dark eyes. Fear and desperation were stamped on her face.

As he stared at her, Griffin hesitated. Why the hell was he drawing this shit out? She was a vamp, he'd caught her feeding, so he should have staked her already.

No. Not…her.

The human Griffin had nearly forgotten staggered to his feet. "Wh-what happened?" The man's hand rose to his throat. "I'm…bleeding…"

"Get the hell out of here," Griffin barked at him.

The guy started to scurry away.

"Good Samaritan," Isabella murmured. "That man was going to attack me in this alley. What if I *had* been a human woman? What then?"

Fuck.

Griffin looked over his shoulder. The jerk was running now. Getting away…

Griffin gave chase. Griffin yanked the stake away from his vamp and ran after the human. The fool never stood a chance. Griffin caught him within seconds. Griffin dragged the fellow up against him. *"Never touch another."*

"What? Man, I'm *bleeding!* I need a hospital—"

"Your knife is in that alley." He'd watched Isabella toss the knife away as if it hadn't mattered. It did matter. "Your prints are all over it. It's the knife you put to a woman's throat tonight. You think I'll forget you? I'll *never* forget you. Don't touch another woman. Don't even think of hurting—"

A knife's sharp blade sank into Griffin. It pierced deep into his chest, and then it twisted.

The human he held *smiled* at Griffin. *"Fucker,"* the bastard grunted. "I always have a second weapon."

Griffin felt the blood pouring from his chest. From his heart. Smoke rose from the wound.

The asshole human ran away. Griffin staggered, trying to go after him, but the knife...shit, had that been a *silver* blade? *I'm burning because of the silver.* His knees gave way, and Griffin hit the ground. He grabbed the hilt of the knife and yanked it out—

"That's an awful lot of blood." *Isabella.*

His head tilted back. Griffin stared up at her.

"I think he hit your heart." She knelt in front of him. Her hands rose and pressed to his wound. "Bet you're wishing you'd let me drain him about now, aren't you?"

Pain shuddered through him. "What…are you…doing…?"

"Believe it or not, I'm trying to help you." She exhaled on a heavy sigh. "I don't know what you are, but that wound is really bad. Most wouldn't survive it." She pressed her lips together and then said, "But I can make sure you keep living."

Oh, hell—

She lifted her wrist to her mouth and bit down. Then she put her bloody wrist to his mouth. "You won't get any diseases or infections from me. My blood will just give you a power boost. You'll heal fast, and then you can go right back to saving the world…or whatever it is that you do."

Drinking her blood? No, no, that was absolutely forbidden by his kind. He could not—

Griffin fell back, his shoulders hitting the ground. He had plenty of healing powers on his own, but silver was toxic to his kind, and a silver knife to the heart? *Shit, but I'm in trouble.* His mouth had gone dry. His fingers felt numb. He tried to speak, but couldn't.

"I won't watch you die. Not while I can help." Once more, Isabella put her wrist to his lips. "Don't worry, you won't change. You're not going to wake up as a vampire." She gave him a sad smile. "I was born this way."

What?

Her blood trickled past his lips. Griffin swallowed, automatically, and as her blood hit his system...

His claws burst out. Fur exploded along his skin. His body began to contort. His bones popped and snapped.

"You're a werewolf!" Her cry was horrified, but she didn't pull her hand away from his mouth. She kept giving him her precious blood.

She kept wrecking his whole world.

Forbidden. Stop. Breaking all the rules. Turn away...

His wound was healing. His heart was racing fast—strong and powerful now. But his entire focus—even as his beast clawed for his freedom—his entire focus was on the sexy little vampire before him. The woman who'd just sealed both of their fates.

He looked at her—and saw everything. Every. Fucking. Thing.

He could smell her sweet scent. It flooded his being. Flowers. Woman. Sex.

He could hear her heart beating. Drumming too fast because she *was* afraid. And, unbelievably, his own heart shuddered as it fought to match her rhythm. His left-hand—now tipped with deadly claws—reached for her.

And his mouth tightened on her wrist. His teeth sank into her skin. Her blood poured into his mouth and every precious, delicious drop made him stronger. Primed him. Tuned him…to her.

"Th-that's enough."

He kept drinking. Her blood was in him. *She* was in him. Did she realize…there was now no escape for her? Wherever she went, he'd find her. Always.

"Let go. You have enough."

He'd never have enough of her. She'd seen to that. They were both cursed. In hell, together. And things were only about to get worse. For both of them.

Isabella shoved hard against him. He let her go even as a growl broke from him. He couldn't hold back the transformation. Griffin's beast was too strong. His hands slammed into the cracked pavement as he gave himself up to his wolf.

Her footsteps thundered away from him as she ran. As if she could get away. Wherever she went, wherever she hid…he'd track her.

Because she was his.

CHAPTER TWO

Her wrist was burning. The wound had healed—Isabella always healed incredibly fast—but she could still *feel* his mouth on her, like some sort of brand that had gone beneath her skin.

She'd run through the city, constantly looking over her shoulder. She'd been terrified she'd see the beast coming after her.

A werewolf. Oh, jeez. Isabella had never encountered a werewolf before. She'd actually hoped they were all long gone from this world. From the time she'd been a little girl, her family had always told her how dangerous—how uncontrollable—a werewolf could be.

Stay away from the beasts. They'll gobble up girls like you.

And one *had* tried to gobble her up. He'd taken her blood. Taken and taken when she'd just been trying to help him. What an ungrateful beast.

She yanked open the door to her hotel room. A fancy place in one of the bustling casinos, the room had seemed like a haven to her when she'd first arrived in town. She'd come to Vegas because it was a tourist hotspot. What better place to disappear? Only…

No one told me there were werewolves in Sin City. That little detail had been missing from the travel guides.

She kicked the hotel room door shut behind her and ran for the closet. It was a swanky room. The best she'd been able to afford because she'd been treating herself. Now, though, it was time to ditch the swankiness and get as far from Vegas as possible. She started throwing her clothes into her bag. Shoving in her shoes and —

A knock sounded at her door.

Isabella froze. Whoever was knocking…*Please, please, don't be the big, bad wolf.* She edged toward the door.

The knock came again.

Would a werewolf bother knocking? She didn't think so. Wouldn't he just kick in the door if he were there?

They'll gobble up girls like —

A man's voice called, "Ms. Abandonato? It's the hotel manager. I want to make sure your room is to your liking."

Her room? A bit dazed, she glanced around. Her wrist kept throbbing.

There was a pause from the other side of the door. "Is everything okay?" the manager asked.

No, the world was absolutely not okay.

Isabella put her eye to the peephole and glanced into the hallway. A tall, thin male stood on the other side of her door. His hair was combed back from his high forehead, and the light gleamed off his round glasses.

Not my werewolf.

Fumbling, Isabella yanked open the door.

He smiled at her. "I saw you go into your room, so I thought this would be a perfect time to check on you."

"It's not perfect. I can't talk now." Not when there was so much running to do.

"I only need a moment." His bright blue gaze swept over her, and his stare stilled on her shirt front. "I think you've hurt yourself," he murmured. "There's blood on your clothes."

Her gaze fell to her shirt. "N-not my blood—"

He hit her—shoved both of his hands against her shoulders and pushed her back into the room. "No," his voice had gone hard and cold. "I suspected it wasn't." Then he pulled a gun from his pocket.

Isabella stared at him with wide eyes. "Who are you?"

Definitely *not* the hotel manager. But then, she should have noticed sooner that the guy wasn't wearing the standard uniform that she'd seen on the other staff members.

"I'm Felix Flemming, and I've been waiting a long time for you."

Her gaze darted from the gun to his face. "Buddy, I don't know you, and I'm having a really bad night so —"

"Blood loss will make your kind weak. I can fill your body full of bullets and let you bleed out on the floor. Then, when you're helpless, I can have my team come up and carry you out of here. That's one option."

Your kind. Her shoulders tensed.

"The first couple of experiments were failures for me. But I have high hopes about tonight." The guy who'd identified himself as Felix smiled at her. "My bait contacted me and told me about the developments in the alley. I'm very, *very* pleased. And because of that fact, we can try to do things the easy way. You can come with me willingly…"

Go with him? Um, the hell, no.

"Or I can fill your body with bullets." His smile was evil. "Because there is no escape for you. I've got a team of five men waiting in the hallway. Even *if* you were to magically get past me, you'd still have to deal with them."

Not true, jerk. I'd only have to face them if I tried to escape through the hallway. Luckily, she had another plan stirring in her head.

Isabella drew in a slow, deep breath. She let her face soften even as she hunched her shoulders and tried to appear weak. "I'll come willingly." She pulled up her power, knowing she'd only have one good shot at attacking him. She crept toward Felix. "There's just one thing I need first…" Her stare held his.

"What's that?" His eyes were locked with hers.

"For you to drop the fucking gun." Power burned from her. "Drop it, *now*."

Instead of dropping it, he pressed the weapon right to her chest. "You think I don't know about a vamp's compulsion? Why the hell do you think I'm wearing these glasses? Special lenses, my dear. They distort my environment just enough that your magic doesn't work on me."

Oh, shit. "In that case…" Isabella rasped — and then she yanked the weapon from him in a lightning fast move. His fingers squeezed the trigger when she grabbed the gun's barrel, and the bullet blasted, but it missed her. Mostly. She felt the bullet graze her side even as Felix shouted for his men.

Not hesitating, Isabella whirled away from him. She sprinted for the window on the right. She was high up, on the seventh floor, so this wasn't going to be the most pleasant experience of her life.

"Shoot her!" Felix yelled. *"Stop her!"*

Gunfire erupted.

She flew *into* the window. It was probably supposed to be reinforced glass or something but…*not paranormal proof.* She took that whole pane of glass out with her hit, and then she was plummeting down, down, falling straight to the earth below. The sidewalk came up to meet her in a blinding, sickening swirl, and then she hit it. The impact knocked the breath from her, and Isabella was pretty sure it shattered her bones, too.

For a time, the entire world went dark. Everything was covered in a blanket of black.

Isabella had a little secret. She might be a vampire, but she was still afraid of the dark. She was afraid of a whole lot of things.

"I think she's dead!" A woman's high-pitched, horrified voice penetrated the darkness.

Isabella sucked in a breath—vampires actually did need to breathe. Their hearts beat, blood flowed in their bodies—they were *undead,* not dead, after all—and she pushed herself up. Her arm felt funny. So did her leg. A quick glance showed they were both broken.

I'll heal. I always do.

Someone screamed, "Oh, my God!" Then a woman with almost white-blonde hair fainted, hitting the ground right next to Isabella.

"Stop her!"

Isabella's head jerked at that blasted order. Gawking humans were staring at her, but over their shoulders, she caught sight of Felix and his goons. They were rushing toward her. So, broken limbs or not, she had to get out of there.

Isabella shoved her broken bones into a semi-correct position and she fled. Every staggering step was absolute torture, but she didn't slow down. She couldn't. Eventually, her body would heal itself. For the moment, though, she had to take the pain—and run.

This night cannot get any worse. And to think, she'd thought Sin City would be fun. How could a woman be more wrong?

***

Griffin followed Isabella's scent to a high-end casino/hotel combo in the heart of Vegas. One filled with about a million glittering lights. It had taken him a bit of time to pursue his prey. He'd needed to get back-up clothes out of his car. Needed to get his beast in serious check.

And I needed to figure out what in the hell I am going to do with her. Because there was one law in the werewolf world. *The vampire is the enemy.* If a wolf encountered a vamp, then the vamp died. No debate. Evil was eradicated.

A crowd had gathered near the front of the glittering building.

"*I thought she was dead!*" A woman's voice rose to reach his ears. An ambulance had pulled up near the casino/hotel's entrance, and an EMT was treating a blonde woman. "She jumped out of that window—had to be seven floors up! When she hit the ground, *I heard her bones snap.*" Dark lines of mascara ran down the blonde's face. "It was *horrible!*"

Griffin stiffened. His gaze lifted, and he saw the gaping hole seven floors up. *Not Isabella, not...*

But his nostrils flared, and he caught the scent of Isabella's blood. It was a scent he now knew all too well. He shoved through the crowd, and sure enough, next to the broken glass on the ground, he saw drops of her blood. And he *knew* it was Isabella's blood. The scent was instantly recognizable. Imprinted on his very soul.

Isabella had jumped from the window. Isabella's bones had snapped. Isabella had—

"*She got up!*" the woman cried. "And she ran away. How did she do that? How is that even possible? How—"

Griffin's head turned toward the ambulance.

"Probably just a publicity stunt, ma'am," the EMT assured her. "You know the magicians around here are always pulling shit like this. Now, you just take it easy..."

Isabella's fall had been no publicity stunt. Why had she leapt from seven stories?

Fear grew within him. It took a moment for Griffin to recognize the emotion because it had been far too long since he'd feared anyone or anything.

Find her. Protect her.

He backed away from the crowd. Isabella's scent was faint on the breeze, so he knew she'd raced from the scene. She'd run while she'd been hurt. His steps picked up speed. He would find her. He had to find her.

If another werewolf in the city got to Isabella before he did…

The vampire is the enemy.

No, he *would* get to Isabella first.

CHAPTER THREE

She had to feed. Dammit. Isabella slapped her hands against the dirty brick wall on the outside of a blaring bar. She was far away from the main Vegas strip, on a side of town that tourists wouldn't visit. Music blasted, the scent of cigarettes drifted in the air, and her whole body trembled.

She'd used too much energy running—and then healing. Now her bones were back in the right place and her cuts had mended, but she staggered with each step she took. If she didn't feed soon, Isabella knew she'd be passing out. She had to find prey, fast.

Her eyes squeezed shut. She could do this. She could walk up to the bouncer, give him a smile, compel him, and get her ass in that bar. Once inside, she'd find some drunk asshole to be her lucky victim. Easy. Maybe.

A rich, woodsy scent teased her nose. She pushed away from the wall and swung toward—

"Going somewhere?"

Her knees almost buckled. It was the werewolf. Only he was looking a whole lot less *beast-mode.* He'd reverted back to his human form. His hair was dark, his eyes a vivid green, and his face…beneath the flickering street lamp, he looked scary as hell.

Scary not like a wolf, but like…like the kind of trouble a smart woman steered clear of. Dangerous, bad, *sexy* scary.

He was tall, with wide, strong shoulders. His shoulders stretched the fabric of the black t-shirt he wore. A pair of jeans hung low on his hips, and boots covered his feet. She didn't even know how the guy had gotten new clothes so soon. The last time she'd seen him, he'd been ripping through the garments he wore. Literally tearing them to shreds with his claws.

He took a step toward her.

Isabella immediately backed up. "Stay away from me!"

He stilled. "I'm not going to hurt you."

They were on the side of the bar, on a street that looked empty, and she knew better than to believe his lies. "So says the *werewolf.*" She licked her lips because they were desert dry.

His gaze immediately fell to her mouth and…heated?

Why was his gaze warming while he stared at her lips?

She threw out her hand and hit the brick wall, steadying herself right before her knees would have buckled.

"You're…hurt. I smell the blood on you."

"Right, well, that happens when you jump from a seventh floor window." Her breath rasped out. "But don't worry. I'm all healed. No more wounds." *Just weakness. A weakness that will go away when I get a little liquid power in me.*

He took another step toward her.

"No! I said *stay away, werewolf!*"

"I'm not a threat to you." His voice was deep and rumbling, and it seemed to sink right beneath her skin. "And in case you missed it when we met before, my name's Griffin."

No, she hadn't missed it. She hadn't missed anything about him. Her wrist throbbed. Burned. That was so *weird*. The closer he got to her, Isabella swore she could feel his bite actually warming her skin. "You're not a threat?" Isabella lifted her chin. "My mistake. I wrongly assumed the guy who tried to *stake* me before might be dangerous."

He growled.

She shivered. *Why am I shivering? Growls aren't sexy. This guy isn't sexy. He's probably a werewolf psychopath!*

"Things are…different now."

Isabella had no idea what that was supposed to mean. "Just get out of my way, okay? You say you're no threat. Fine. If that's the case, then leave. Because I've got places to go." *And people to bite.*

Instead of leaving, she blinked and the guy was right in front of her. Griffin reached out and his fingers curled beneath her chin. As soon as he touched her, a surge of electricity pulsed through her entire body. She found herself gasping, and—very, very embarrassingly—her nipples hardened. She also realized that rich, woodsy scent that she'd detected moments before? It was coming from him. A wild scent...an oddly alluring scent.

"Your heart is beating too slowly."

"You can hear that?" And she'd thought she had good hearing...

"Werewolf senses, sweetheart."

Since *when* was she sweetheart?

"Your breathing is labored, and you're trembling." Griffin lightly stroked her chin with his thumb. "Why did you jump? Were you so upset by what happened between us that you thought the only alternative was—"

"You're insane." Isabella just broke right through his words because she'd come to that important realization—*the werewolf is crazy.* "I *jumped* because some assholes with guns broke into my hotel room and tried to kidnap me. The only way to escape happened to be through my window."

A faint furrow appeared between his brows.

Her gaze dropped to his throat. "What I wouldn't give for a taste," she whispered as she stumbled toward him.

Quite a few things happened then...

Griffin swore and pulled her...*closer.*

Footsteps raced toward them.

A man shouted, *"I see her!"*

And bullets blasted into the night.

Isabella opened her mouth, prepared to scream as those bullets sank into her. The assholes had found her. As weak as she was, they were going to take her. She was helpless.

But the werewolf lifted her into his arms and he *leapt* up into the air. The move was insane, so incredibly fast, and Isabella was sure she felt the heat of the bullets race by her skin—yet those bullets didn't strike her.

Because of him.

Griffin touched down on the roof of the bar. She was still held in his arms, gaping at him in surprise. He'd just saved her ass, big time. He leaned his head close to hers, putting his lips just an inch, maybe two, from hers. "They're dead," he promised.

It took her a moment to process what he'd said. And when she did, it was too late. He'd already let her go. He placed her on the roof and then he leapt back down to the street below. She blinked after him, then screamed, *"No!"* because she didn't want to see the wolf get his body riddled with bullets.

But as she watched, clinging desperately to the edge of that roof, he went right for his enemies. There were two humans there. One fired at him, but Griffin dodged the bullet and then his claws swiped at the man who'd just tried to kill him.

The shooter went down. He didn't get up.

The guy's partner aimed —

"Look out, Griffin!" Isabella yelled.

He turned at her shout. A bullet grazed his shoulder. It didn't slow him down. He leapt at the shooter before the man could fire a second time. The human hit the ground.

Two dead bodies.

So much blood.

Then Griffin looked up at her. His eyes were glowing. His face was harsher, sharper than before. He appeared as a combination of man and beast, and fear clawed at Isabella's insides. She whipped around and scrambled across that roof.

He's too comfortable with death. He's too dangerous. He's...

In front of her. He was right in front of her, again. Griffin was standing right in front of her and his hands — tipped with razor sharp claws — were reaching for her.

Those same claws had just killed two men.

"I told you," he said, "they're dead."

She gaped at him.

He frowned. "You're welcome."

He expected her to thank him for death? Was the guy straight-up crazy? Wait, yes, they'd already established that he was.

"You'll come with me now," Griffin said.

"No, I won't." He didn't know her. Didn't know about her strict *no killing* rule. And he didn't know how close she was to a serious freak-out. "Go away, wolf. How many times…" Weakness weighed down her limbs. "Do I have to say…go away?"

"The humans in the bar heard the gunshots. Cops will be called. Do you want to be here when they swarm the scene?"

No, she wanted to be far away.

He pulled her into his arms. Held her. Seemed…oddly happy. "You fit me."

Crazy werewolf. Her eyes were on his throat. One bite, just one…a few sips of blood and she'd be back to her normal power level. She'd be able to get away from him.

"I was told…it was wrong. Taboo. It's not." He turned his head. His glowing eyes met hers. "*We're* not. I'll fight anyone who challenges my right to you."

Yes, well… "I'm sorry that you're crazy." His throat was just too close—and if she didn't get blood soon, she'd be passing out. "May I bite you?"

He blinked. "You bite me, and we're going to fuck. I want you too badly."

Uh…

He leapt off the roof. Since she'd recently taken a fall that ended with broken bones, Isabella immediately closed her eyes. She wasn't in the mood for more pain.

She didn't get pain.

They didn't crash into the ground. He landed on his feet, not even swaying a little bit. He held her easily in his arms. Her eyes opened as Griffin ran past the dead men, and then he was snaking through twists and turns in the city, stopping right next to a motorcycle. He put her on the seat and climbed on before her.

"Werewolves ride motorcycles?" Isabella shook her head.

"Hell, yeah, they do. But this one isn't mine. So give me a second to get her going."

Not...his? She realized he was hot-wiring the ride. The werewolf was a killer *and* a thief. And he'd saved her ass. The motorcycle growled to life.

"Hold on. *Tight.*"

She could barely stay upright. And he wanted her holding on? The motorcycle lurched forward, and her hands flew around him. She held him tight as the wind whipped against her body.

The bloodlust grew within her. She needed to drink. The weakness was getting worse. The buildings and the people all passed her in a blur. Her entire focus was on him. She could feel the beating of his heart. His body emitted a warmth that drew her in, and the werewolf smelled absolutely...delicious.

She leaned forward, pressing her body up against his. They weren't wearing helmets, probably because he hadn't been able to steal those. He braked at a red light. Her tongue slipped out and licked along the edge of his neck.

"Sweetheart…" The endearment came out as a warning. "You are playing with fire."

Her head turned. There was a club just a few feet away, right past the curb. Fast, techno music blared from inside what was no doubt a hot-spot. She could see bodies gyrating inside. "I'll get off here," she whispered. "And just grab a quick drink." And she did. She jumped off the bike, but nearly fell. She managed to stay upright, but he grabbed her wrist.

"You're going to drink…from another?"

Hadn't she just said that? Her eyes narrowed on him. Griffin had no idea how dangerous bloodlust could be for her. If she didn't drink soon, she might lose her control. She might hurt her prey.

A car horn blared behind them.

Griffin ignored the driver. "You want to drink, then you drink from me."

"The price is too high." Because his words kept playing in her head, over and over. *We'll fuck.* A werewolf lover would savage her. If only half of the stories she'd heard about his kind were true…

She fell. Her strength gave way even as her fangs slipped out completely. Before she could hit the ground, he'd scooped her up and put her on the motorcycle again. Only this time, she was in front of him, with the warmth of his body surrounding her. The motorcycle shot forward into the night.

"You're weak."

Ah, now he was catching on. "Must...have...blood..."

"You drank earlier." His voice rose over the purr of that bike. "I saw you feed on that bastard in the alley."

Her tongue slid over one fang. "That was before...broke bones...had to...heal, inside and out." Because she'd had some fun, internal injuries after her fall, too.

He swore—using some truly, wickedly inventive words. Then his right wrist flew up. His left hand kept a steady hold on the handlebar. "I can't believe I'm saying this shit, but take my blood."

"No, I won't—"

"We're not fucking on the bike. The fucking will wait until I have you alone, not on a damn street."

Uh...good to know?

"I won't have you weak. Not while I can help you." His voice seemed to vibrate behind her. "Consider it payback."

His wrist was in front of her mouth, and Isabella didn't have the willpower to stop herself. She needed blood, and she wasn't going to be fool enough to turn him away.

She licked his skin.

He swore again. The guy had a tendency to cuss far too much.

Her fangs sank into him.

"Fucking hell." Yet Griffin didn't sound like he meant those words. His growled voice hadn't contained pain. Only pleasure.

His blood slipped onto her tongue, and a white-hot desire exploded in her body.

Fucking hell, indeed.

CHAPTER FOUR

"This is kidnapping."

The woman was too tempting. Just staring at her made him ache. She'd had his blood — a bite that had brought him to the brink of orgasm even as he'd been riding a damn motorcycle — and now she stood before him, no longer weak. Golden skin practically glowing, dark hair falling around her face all sexy and tousled-like because of their frantic ride through the city, lips red and full…

She waved her hand in front of his face. "Are you listening to me? You can't keep me here. This. Is. Kidnapping." She glanced around, frowning. "And it's kidnapping by keeping me in a way shady place."

His back teeth locked. "It's my office." And yeah, it was a bit shady. So he hadn't exactly gotten a cleaning lady in the place in, oh, forever. He didn't usually cater to high end clients. He liked the rougher jobs. The wilder ones. They satisfied his beast.

She moved to stand behind the desk. Her fingers slid over the old wood. "This is where you work? When you're not, you know, plotting to kill helpless vamps?"

He looked down at his wrist. Her bite mark had already faded. No one had ever warned him that a vamp's bite would feel so good. His kind healed incredibly fast, and he actually regretted that fact right then — he would have liked wearing her mark. Strange, though, because even though the mark had faded, Griffin could have sworn he could still feel the heat of her bite...*beneath* his skin.

She jumped up on his desk. *Sat* on the damn thing like she owned it and started swaying her feet. *Bare* feet, by the way. He'd only noticed her lack of shoes when he'd braked in front of his office. He had no idea where the woman's sexy high heels were. A rather unfortunate loss. He would have loved seeing her in those killer red heels and nothing else.

"Do you routinely try to stake vamps? Is that like...your job? Or just your hobby?"

He stalked toward her. As he closed in, Isabella stiffened. She pulled her lower lip between her teeth, and her gaze darted over him. He didn't stop walking until he was right in front of her, and then Griffin put his hands on either side of her body, trapping her there on his desk. "I was told you were a killer."

She gave a quick, nervous laugh. "Total lie. You saw that I didn't kill anyone tonight."

He didn't laugh. "The guy who came to me was certain that you were attacking men, and then I saw you myself in that alley. You acted as bait, right? Luring your prey to you. The fool thought you were vulnerable, and then you attacked him."

Her delicate jaw hardened. "First of all, I don't kill my donors."

Donors?

"I try to target jerks who deserve to be bitten, and I leave them with a compulsion to *never* hurt another woman again. I try to change them, okay? I try to stop some of the badness in this world. I have to feed or I die. It's not like I chose this life."

"Right. You said you were born this way." Talk about rare. Born vampires were usually the stuff of legends.

"Yes. I'm one hundred percent natural..." Isabella paused. "Vampire."

Griffin only grunted. His fingers slid closer to her body. "Just how long ago were you born, Isabella?"

"I look good for my age." Her response was curt.

He smiled. From where he was standing... "Damn good."

Her gaze lowered.

His thumbs brushed over the outside of her thighs. "You don't need to lie."

And her gaze flew right back up to his.

"Vamps kill. You think I can't handle that truth about you? You're my mate. Not like I have a damn bit of say in this thing between us —"

"Whoa! Stop! Right there. Just stop." Her hands flew up and slammed against his chest. "Back up. Did you just say I was your *mate?*"

He didn't remember stuttering. "It's done. No changing it, not for either of us. We'll just have to deal with the fallout."

Her lips parted. Then closed. Then parted again so that he could see the oddly sexy edge of her sharp, little fangs. "You wanted to kill me tonight. You had a *stake.*"

True. "So we didn't have the most romantic start."

"You're a *werewolf.*"

"Guilty."

"Werewolves might do the whole mating-until-death bit, but vamps don't. Mostly because we don't *die*. I'll be running around long after you're dust."

No, she wouldn't. "Mate."

"*Stop* saying that!" And she shoved him, hard.

If she were dealing with a lesser paranormal, he would have stumbled back at her shove. Lucky for her, he wasn't lesser. He'd be a strong, fit mate for her...forever. "There hasn't been a pairing like ours for a very long time. But be warned. Some will come for us — some on your side, some on mine. They'll probably try to kill us both."

"Get away from me."

"I won't let them hurt you." His voice deepened as he stared down at her. Her sweet scent filled his lungs. "I will fucking *destroy* anyone who tries to hurt you. Our lives are entwined now. There is no going back."

But she shook her head. "Are you…crazy? I feared this before, and you're just making me more convinced than ever."

His gaze focused on her mouth. They'd exchanged bites—they'd *mated,* but he hadn't kissed her yet. That seemed so wrong to him.

"Vampires and werewolves can't mate." Her words came out fast and angry. "We're natural enemies, or did you miss that memo? I've spent my whole life being told to run when I saw a big, bad beast—"

"You can't run from me." Not now. "We're linked by the bite. Anywhere you go, I'd follow."

"Werewolves *kill* my kind."

His hand lifted and curled under her chin. There had been fear in her voice. He couldn't have that. "This werewolf wants to kiss you."

And he did.

His head lowered slowly toward hers. His mouth brushed across her lips. It was a gentle kiss. Careful. Tentative.

He was damn well *not* the tentative type. But she was different. What they would have together would be different, and he didn't want to screw things up more than he already had. So Griffin kept the kiss careful.

Then she licked his lower lip.

He jerked in surprise.

"Oh, jeez, I didn't mean to do that—" Isabella told him, the words low and husky.

She didn't get the chance to say more. His tongue was in her mouth. He was tasting her, he was freaking savoring her, and the desire that the mating bite had created for him—it exploded in a molten need that seemed to burn him from the inside out.

Isabella didn't shove him away. Her arms wrapped around him as she yanked him closer. Her legs flew up and locked around his hips. His dick was long and rock hard, eager to plunge into her and claim the mate he'd never expected.

Vampires and werewolves...the bite had been taboo.

They'd broken the most sacred rule of his kind, and Griffin didn't care. He just wanted her naked. He wanted *in* her. And he wanted—

He heard the thud of footsteps outside of his office door. He caught the wild scent of a wolf, and Griffin jerked away from Isabella as a snarl broke from his lips.

For a moment, she stared at him, appearing absolutely horrified. "What happened? Why the *hell* did I just do that—"

He whirled away from her.

His office door flew inward, propelled by one very hard kick.

"*Vampire!*" The roar came from the werewolf standing in Griffin's doorway. A werewolf who was as tall and just as muscled as Griffin. The werewolf was still in human form, but his claws were out, and the light of a killing fury blazed in his eyes. He lunged forward, no doubt intending to follow Isabella's scent and attack—

Griffin planted himself directly in his pack mate's path. "Carter, stand the hell down." His breath heaved in and out. Griffin's claws were ready to rip and tear.

Carter Sinclair blinked at him. "The woman in here..." His words were guttural. "She's a vamp."

Isabella cleared her throat from behind Griffin. "Wonderful," she announced. "*Two* of you."

Carter leapt forward. Griffin slammed the guy back—only he slammed so hard that Carter hit the floor. "*Stand down!*"

Carter shoved his too-long, blond hair out of his face and jumped right back to his feet. "Are you *insane?* There's a vamp behind you! I'm trying to save your ass!"

The guy had no clue. When the fool made another attempt to get at Isabella, Griffin drove his fist into Carter's face. The werewolf's nose broke and blood spattered.

The nose would heal, of course, eventually.

"What the fuck?" Carter swiped out with his claws.

Griffin easily avoided them. He was faster than Carter. And he didn't want to have to knock out his friend, but—"You don't hurt her. *No one does.*"

Carter stilled. His face went slack with shock. The blood dripped down from his nose. "What have you done?"

Before Griffin could answer, glass shattered. He spun around and saw that Isabella had just leapt from his window. He had one moment to be grateful that his office was on the second floor— *not the seventh this time!* Griffin rushed to the window and caught a glimpse of her running away. Running—and jumping on the motorcycle he'd stolen before. *"Isabella!"*

She paused and looked up at him. Even from a distance, he could see the fear on her face.

He started to leap after her.

"The hell you will!" Carter grabbed his arm and spun Griffin back around. "Want to tell me why you're trying to protect a vamp? Why her scent is all over you? Why—"

The motorcycle's engine growled to life. *Dammit.*

She was getting away.

Or trying to.

"Because she's mine." And that was all he had time to say. He jumped through that window, determined to get his mate back. He hurtled through the air and when he touched down on the cement, his knees didn't even buckle. Then he ran after her.

**

Carter Sinclair swiped away the blood that was dripping onto his mouth. He stared out of the broken window, his stomach in knots. His friend was gone—rushing after the dark-haired vamp. Not even looking back. Griffin had *shifted* as he'd hunted her. The guy had just changed right in the street. That shit was against their laws.

But it seemed Griffin might be doing more than just breaking the old werewolf rule about not shifting when humans were near. It was possible…it was possible that Griffin had just broken one of the oldest laws their kind had…

Never mate a vampire.

Carter's fingers were shaking as he pulled out his phone. He called his alpha, dialing quickly. Griffin was his friend. Hell, the guy was more like a brother most days, *not* just a pack mate. But the vamp's scent had been all over Griffin. And he'd fought to protect the vamp, then gone freaking wild when she'd escaped him.

The phone was answered on the second ring. Jaw locking, Carter said, "Alpha, we have a very big problem."

CHAPTER FIVE

A girl knew when she was being hunted, and Isabella was absolutely certain a predator had her in his sights. She drove until just before dawn, then she took refuge in a no-tell-motel in the middle of the desert. The light from the sun was just streaking across the sky — that little streak was all that she could ever see. Vamps and daylight definitely didn't mix.

Because she was desperate for shelter, Isabella used her power and pushed a compulsion on the young, pimply check-in clerk…and he gave her a free room. Since she didn't have a single dime on her, she'd needed that room, so Isabella only felt vaguely guilty for using her gift on the human. She tended not to use her power too much because of, well, unfortunate past experiences.

She tried to be good. She really did. Some days — some nights, rather — it was just hard to toe the line.

Isabella locked the thin motel door behind her. Then she yanked the dusty cover off the bed and hung it over the lone window in the room, hoping for a bit more protection from the sun. The sun was poison for her kind. If she got too much of it, then Isabella would be getting one very serious sunburn—the kind that ended with her being ash that floated in the wind.

When she'd made sure to cover every available inch of that window, Isabella collapsed onto the bed. It sagged beneath her, but she didn't care. She was far away from the crazy werewolf. She was out of the sun. And she was safe, for the moment.

She just wasn't sure how long that safety would last.

Her eyes closed.

And her wrist throbbed from a bite that had healed hours ago. Impossible.

Mate.

He was wrong. A heavy, drugging weariness pulled at her. The higher the sun rose, the weaker she would become. That weakness was such a danger for her kind. She was always at her most vulnerable when the sun brightened the sky.

The werewolf had found her before. Would he find her again? Surely not. She'd driven so far. She'd—

A knock sounded at her door. She forced her heavy eyelids open.

"Sweetheart…" That was *his* voice. *Griffin.* "Open the door. I know you're in there."

She didn't move off the bed. No, no, he *couldn't* be out there. And she couldn't let him in.

She was too weak already. If she let him in now, she would be defenseless against him. The werewolf could kill her.

"If you don't let me in…" What could have been laughter slid beneath his words. "Then I'll just huff and puff…"

Her hand fisted around the sheet, jerking it away from the mattress.

"And I'll break the door down." He knocked again, harder this time.

Her whole body seemed sluggish. Isabella tried to push herself up, but instead of rising, she just flopped off the bed and hit the floor with a heavy *thunk*.

"Isabella?" Alarm sharpened his voice. Then he was breaking down the door. She heard the weak wood splinter and sunlight poured into the room. Because she was on the floor near the side of the bed, the light didn't hit her, but she still let out a quick cry.

Immediately, he was in front of her. Griffin was wearing mismatched clothes and frowning at her. His hands reached out to her. "Isabella—"

"Don't…hurt me." She hated begging him, but there was no choice. She could barely move at all any longer. *I hate the sun so much.*

He blinked. "Hurt you?"

Her lashes began to close.

"Sweetheart, I will *never* hurt you. I swear that on my own life." He lifted her up with hands that were far too gentle to belong to a werewolf.

He rose, with her cradled against his chest, and she could hear the soothing rhythm of his heartbeat. "Guess this part of the old story is true, huh? The day is your most dangerous time."

He put her in the middle of the bed. She heard the floor creak, and then the door squeaked as it was…closed?

She managed to crack open one eye and saw that, yes, he'd shut the door. He'd even put a chair under the broken part to help hold the door in place.

And he was stalking back toward her.

The bed sagged even more when he slid in beside her. His hands reached out, and Griffin pulled her against his body. He was so warm. Strong.

Safe.

No, no, that's a lie. There's no way I can find safety with someone like him.

"You sleep. I'll watch over you during the day." His lips pressed to her cheek. "That's the way it was so long ago, right? And I guess that's what will happen for us."

Watching…over her? No, no one ever watched over her. She was on her own. Had been for far too long. She didn't have a family. She didn't have friends. Not anymore. They'd all turned their backs on her. She was the freak. She was the broken one. Her own kind had tried to kill her.

But a werewolf was holding her in his arms. He was keeping her close. Impossibly, she found her breath easing into the rhythm of her deepest sleep as she finally let the last bit of her control go.

And she slept, cradled close by the man who should have been her mortal enemy.

***

Carter marched into the motorcycle shop. Silence greeted him, and all the werewolves assembled…shit, their eyes were cold. He saw flashes of fang and the curve of razor sharp claws. All of the beasts were close to the surface. With damn good reason.

"Speak." It was the pack leader's voice — booming out and echoing around the garage. The place was a chop shop some days and a semi-legitimate business on others. It was also werewolf central in Vegas because the motorcycle gang leader — he was also the leader of their pack. Vane Bollen stood in the middle of that shop, his arms crossed over his chest, and his long, black hair brushing over his shoulders. Tattoos covered his arms — tattoos in the shapes of wild wolves running beneath the moon.

Even on good days, Carter found Vane to be an arrogant asshole. But the guy had been pack leader when Carter rolled into town, and pack law *was* pack law. Carter exhaled on a hard breath. "There's a new vamp in town."

Vane laughed. "So? Griffin takes care of them."

Yes, normally, he did. Griffin was Vane's enforcer. From what Carter had seen, Griffin normally did all the dirty work, while Vane took the credit for the pack's tough-as-nails reputation. "Not this time."

There were murmurs from behind him.

Some of the smugness left Vane's face. "What?"

"He was..." Shit, he felt like such a total traitor. Carter's gaze jerked around the shop. Maybe he was wrong. Maybe...

"*What* was Griffin doing?" Vane demanded. Then, before Carter could speak, Vane bounded forward. He grabbed Carter's shirt-front. "*Your* blood?"

Yes, it was. He was a bit of a bleeder. "Griffin fought me."

More murmurs. Werewolves could be some gossipy bastards.

"Why?" Vane's fangs were lengthening. His brown eyes were gleaming with the power of a wolf.

Carter swallowed. *This was such a mistake.* But... "Promise we help Griffin. I've heard of this happening — it was just a long fucking time ago, but I heard the stories. If we can separate them, promise we'll help Griffin." Because that was what he wanted to do. He wanted to help his friend.

Help Griffin, not hurt him. *Not* kill him.

"Why does Griffin need help?" Vane's voice boomed.

No one was murmuring any longer. They were all too busy waiting for Carter's response. Dammit. "Because he was protecting the vamp. He was fighting me...for her."

And the garage erupted with howls of fury.

***

Isabella's eyes flew open. Scared, frantic, her gaze jerked to the left—and she saw the peeling paint on the wall. Then she rolled, turning her body to the right and saw—

A big, naked werewolf.

"That's good to know," Griffin murmured, his voice low and sexy and rumbling straight through her body. "You don't wake up slowly. It's fast—just bam, the sun sets and you're back with me."

Back with him? "Why are you in bed with me?"

"Because it was easier to hold you this way?"

She sat up, fast, and yanked the thin sheet up with her. Then Isabella realized she was still wearing her clothes.

He lifted one dark brow. "I took off my own clothes—I like to sleep in the nude, for future reference—but stripping you while you were unconscious wasn't exactly the move of a gentleman."

She licked her lips. His gaze followed that movement and heated.

Hello, trouble.

Isabella cleared her throat. "Is that what you are? Some kind of gentleman werewolf?"

He laughed. The sound was deep and rumbly and for some reason, it made her heart feel warm.

"Hardly, sweetheart."

"Stop calling me that," she muttered. "Like *now*." The endearment was a lie. She hated lies. She'd spent decades with too many lies.

"I'm not exactly known as a good guy in wolf circles." He turned onto his side and the sheet had dropped very, very far on him. *Mostly because I snatched it from him.* But his part of the sheet dipped far enough for her to see the rippling muscles of his six pack. Twelve pack? Far enough for her to see the faint edge of —

"I can get rid of the sheet, if you want," he offered. "My body is yours."

She needed to get out of that bed. She needed to stop gaping at him. Her gaze rose, but then her eyes were just caught by his tattoos. Dark, swirling tattoos that covered his left arm from shoulder to forearm.

"Special ink." His voice was low. "Had to be special, otherwise, my body just would have pushed the ink right out. These are pack tats. They tell other wolves that I'm a hunter."

The fact that he was a hunter was hardly reassuring.

"I'm guessing you've never fucked a werewolf before."

Her attention snapped back to his face. "No." Not likely, considering she'd been told for most of her life that a wolf would— "Gobble me up," she whispered.

His green eyes—smoldering eyes— narrowed. "What?"

"I was…I was told that werewolves were too dangerous for our kind. When I was a kid…" Now her lips twisted in a mirthless smile. "I was warned never to get close to a werewolf. That you'd gobble me up."

His jaw hardened. "Now that is one fabulous idea. I'd love to put my mouth all over you."

Her heart was jack-hammering in her chest. Her body felt tight and hot, and her nipples pressed against her shirt-front, and they were so sensitive that she almost gasped. "Y-you haven't had sex with a vampire before."

She could see the desire—the lust—in his gaze. "Haven't had that pleasure," Griffin responded. "Yet."

Her stare darted away from his. "Y-you don't want to have sex with me."

His laughter came again. "Trust me, there is nothing I want more right now."

Those deep, sexy words pierced right to her core. Isabella could feel herself getting wet for him—*with just words.* Maybe she'd just gone way too long without sex. Maybe that was it. When *had* she been with a lover last? "I bite," Isabella blurted. That was one of the reasons it had been *forever* since she'd been with a lover. She always ran the risk of killing her human partner. Sex with another vampire wasn't an option because, in general, vamps were too damn possessive and controlling.

"So do I."

Oh. Sweet. Hell. Her gaze collided with his once more, and, this time, Isabella couldn't look away.

"You think I mind your bite?" Griffin shook his head. "Bite all you want, climax all you want…scream my fucking name…*all you want.* I can take everything you have, and I'll just give you *more* in return."

This wasn't happening. She'd woken up and desire had hit her. Not normal. But then, she usually woke up alone, not snuggled with some werewolf. A werewolf who'd just…what? Watched her sleep? That was creepy shit. "What did you do? All the hours I was asleep, what were you doing?"

"Protecting you."

She blinked at his response.

"It's what I'm supposed to do now, isn't it? Because we're mated." Anger came and went, flashing in his eyes. "The way it was so long ago."

"I have no clue what you're talking about. I get that werewolves mate." Even vamps knew that. Werewolves mated *for life*. "But your kind doesn't mate with a vamp. That's not even possible."

His body stiffened. "It's more than possible. It's the way things were done for centuries. Once upon a time, your kind *only* mated with werewolves."

She pressed her back to the headboard. "No, that's not true. Werewolves *hunt* vampires. They stake them—just like you tried to stake me." As soon as she said those words, Isabella jumped from the bed. What in the hell had she been thinking? Had she actually been considering having sex with him? Was she having some kind of breakdown?

"Yes, we hunt, we fight because we're enemies now. But we used to be your protectors." He didn't get out of the bed, but he did sit up. And the sheet dipped even more. He was aroused—heavily aroused. "Who do you think watched over your kind during the day? Who was perfectly designed to protect you? Thanks to some superhuman strength and senses that are ten times stronger than a mortal's, which paranormal was the best suited for the job?"

He was *wrong*. "I've been alive for almost two hundred years. You've been our enemies for all that time."

His smile flashed. "You *do* look good for your age."

"A vamp can't transform a werewolf—it's not like your *mate* could bite you and turn you into—into—"

Griffin shook his head. "A werewolf can never become a vampire. Our genetics don't let us change."

Right. Isabella exhaled on a rough sigh as she tried to figure out this situation. "Then a vamp would have—what? Fifty years with her *mate* before he died? Your kind don't live forever, your kind couldn't—"

"When the mating bites are exchanged, the two souls link. Then the werewolf can live as long as his vampire mate."

When the mating bites are exchanged...

She didn't want to believe his crazy story, but as if on cue, her wrist started to throb. The wrist he'd bitten. She jerked up her hand, staring at the skin. No mark was there, but she could still *feel* him.

"That's right, sweetheart. I bit you, you bit me...it's done. I felt the mating bond set—it *burned* into my skin, and I know you felt it, too."

At any moment, Isabella was sure her heart would burst out of her chest. "Why? *How?*"

"Because you were meant to be mine. I was meant to be yours. Fate. Destiny." He gave her a very wolfish smile. "Doesn't always happen, you know. That was part of the problem. At least, according to the stories I've been told...seems some of *your* kind went on a rampage a few centuries back. They wanted werewolf mates. They *wanted* protectors who would always watch over them, so they rounded up as many werewolves as they could find."

She shook her head. "No." But her voice was weak.

"They took turns biting them, making the werewolves bite vamps, too. They were looking for the mating bond. When it didn't happen, well, it wasn't as if they were just going to let the werewolves walk free — not when the beasts were so damn pissed — and not when they'd gotten a taste for vamp blood."

Her eyes widened. "What do you mean?"

His green gaze slid to her throat. "That's the thing, you see. A vamp's blood tastes real sweet to a werewolf." He licked his lips. "Like delicious candy."

Oh, jeez.

"Vamp blood gives our beasts a rush of power. A surge of strength. It's the best fucking drug in the world."

Her attention shifted to the door. Could she get to that door before he grabbed her? She was fast but...*I think he's faster.*

"So once the vamps had rounded up a mass of wolves — and they didn't find mates in that group that they could use — the vamps decided to pump those werewolves full of silver. After all, they didn't want some blood-lust crazed werewolves attacking them."

"Your story makes no sense." She inched toward the door. "If our blood drives werewolves crazy, then why aren't *you* crazy right now? You had my blood—"

"And it was delicious."

She slipped a bit closer to the door. "But you're not attacking me, and you just said some werewolves mated with vampires, so, of course, they wouldn't have mated if they got all blood crazy—"

"Werewolves stay in control when they are with their mates. *That's* the safety link that must stay in place. But if a werewolf isn't mated to a vampire, there is no control. There is just hunger, the savage need for power." He laughed, and it was a bitter sound. "That's why the mating was so damn dangerous—your kind wanted loyal protectors, but they knew the price they had to pay was their blood. When the bites didn't work, they created ferocious enemies who *only* wanted the vamps' blood."

"A vicious cycle," she whispered. *Another step closer to the door.* "You're saying vamps created their own enemies?"

"The story about werewolves wanting to gobble up the vamps is true. After that first taste, there is no going back for many. Not unless you have your mate."

And he thought she was his mate. That the magical bond had just clicked into place for them.

"You'll never make it."

Isabella froze.

His wolfish smile came again, and this time, she realized he had a dimple in his right cheek. "I'll be on you before you can open the door." He shrugged lazily. "Do you know how far I had to run last night before I caught you? Actually, I ran *and* had to steal another ride—and some poor bastard's clothes. It wasn't a fun night for me, and I don't plan to repeat it tonight."

Her back teeth clenched. "I'm not some defenseless human."

"Never said you were. I just said you'll never make it out the door."

Asshole. She ran for the door. Her fingers shoved away the chair that had been propped beneath the door, then she reached for the broken knob and—

He grabbed her. In an instant, he'd whirled her around and pushed her against the nearest wall, trapping her with his muscled, naked body. "You don't get it, do you, Isabella?" He'd caught her wrists and pushed them over her head, holding them there with one hard hand. "For me...you're it."

"Because you think we're mated? Some magical bond?"

"Some things in this world are magic. I happen to think I'm staring at something pretty fucking magical."

Her gaze fell to his mouth. "You don't know me." Her words were low and husky. "There is nothing magical or good about me. You don't want to be near me. You don't want me to be your mate. You just—you should get as far from me as possible."

His right hand—his free hand—curled around her chin. He tipped back her head, making her stare into his eyes. "You are the thing I want most."

"I'm...I've done bad things." Things that she tried to forget, but couldn't. Vampires weren't exactly built on the *good* side, so his story about her kind basically capturing wolves and then slaughtering the ones that didn't cut it as mates? *Not so far-fetched, unfortunately.* "I've...killed."

His gaze didn't waver.

She felt a tear leak down her cheek. "I didn't want to be this way, okay? When you're born a vampire, the blood hunger is never ending. You don't know anything else. You think that drinking from prey is normal. You don't even realize..." Her words trailed away.

Griffin didn't speak. He just kept watching her with a gaze that seemed to see into her very soul.

"You don't even realize," she made herself say, "how much you're hurting humans." Her family had told her that the prey didn't matter. "They mattered. I could...I could hear their cries even in my sleep. They wouldn't leave me alone. I tried to keep my control, tried not to attack them, I even *starved* myself because I didn't want to bite anyone else, but the need came back. It *always* comes back, even darker and even stronger." Nearly consuming her. "I tried to change my ways. I tried to only go after those who deserve pain of their own...and even then, I swear, I only take a few sips now." Just enough to survive. Enough to keep the darkness at bay so it wouldn't swallow her whole.

As it had once before.

"I'm not here to judge you."

Her lips were trembling. "No? Someone should."

"Then you're looking at the wrong man. I'm not the fucking white knight of the story. I'm not the law. I'm the beast."

His strong body pressed to hers. She could feel the hard length of his arousal.

"I know about the dark." His voice was a growl. "And I know that when I'm near you, it will *never* touch you again."

She wanted to believe him. But no one—*no one*—had ever protected her before. Not until...

Until a werewolf had watched her through the night?

His green gaze seemed to burn. "You can drink from me. It won't hurt me. You won't kill me."

But… "You told me we'd fuck."

He flashed that dimple at her. "You think I can't tell you want me? Sweetheart…"

Now they were back to the endearment.

"I can smell the need on your skin. It's you and it's me here, and it's no one else. You don't need to lie or pretend with me. You *never* need to hide anything from me because I want all of you. Every single part."

It was too fast. Too soon. And the things he was saying—it was as if he'd looked into her very soul and found all of the secrets she kept locked up so tightly. Her hopes and those desperate, foolish dreams. Dreams from a time when she'd thought someone could want a monster.

When someone could love one.

"How about a kiss?" His voice sank through her. "A kiss to prove how much I want you…and how much you want me."

"Is…" She licked her lips and decided she wouldn't lie. Screw it. "Is this need I feel for you real? Or is it all tied up with the bites?" *The biting. The mating. All of the madness.*

"Everything we feel is real. The mating link was nature's way of showing us instantly what it would take our hearts much longer to see on their own."

She wanted that to be true. Foolish hope. It always died last. And...she wanted him. "One kiss." Isabella swallowed. "One kiss and if we don't ignite—"

His laughter stopped her before she could say...*If we don't ignite, then you don't touch me again. I don't touch you. We get this madness under control.*

"We will," Griffin promised her and then his head bent toward hers. His lips pressed to hers. Soft and easy. Gentle, just as he'd been before. It was his gentleness that kept catching her off guard. She expected wildness, savagery. He was a beast, after all. But instead...

His gentleness seemed to melt her heart.

Her lips parted for him. Her tongue swept out and she tasted him, carefully, just as he'd done to her. Hesitantly. Her body trembled. She yearned.

The kiss became deeper. Hotter.

She ignited.

Desire seemed to explode inside of her, and a scorching need burned her from the inside, out. He let go of her hands, and she immediately grabbed him. Her nails sank into his bare shoulders.

Bare.

He was totally naked. She hadn't looked down when he'd first pinned her against the wall, but she'd felt his long length pressing against her. His cock was fully erect as it shoved against her, and she found herself rising onto her tip toes, parting her thighs, wanting to feel him, even closer —

He lifted her up. Held her with the easy strength she knew he possessed. Her skirt hiked up higher — no, he shoved it up higher. His fingers slipped under the edge of her panties, and she heard the silk rip.

The sound just turned her on even more.

It was wrong — what they were doing was *wrong*. He was wrong for her. She was wrong for him. She should stop. She should ignore the desperate need.

But nothing had felt this right to her in a very, very long time. Maybe…never before. Maybe nothing had ever felt this way.

He slid one finger into her, and Isabella almost came. Her body was that tuned, that sensitive. She was already on the verge of release.

"Tell me what you like." His voice was a sensual command. "I will give you *everything*."

Her fangs were stretching. Bloodlust always combined with physical lust for a vampire. She wanted to sink her teeth into him. She wanted to drink from him even as he drove his cock into her. She wanted to feel him deep inside. "M-more…" That was all she could manage to say.

But he gave her more. He slid his finger out, only to work it — and another long, strong finger — back inside of her. His thumb pressed over her clit and her mouth opened in a quick, startled scream.

The orgasm had hit her—that fast. It rolled through her body, making her sex contract greedily around his fingers. Her heart thundered and she wanted...*another. Again. Again!*

"Sweetheart, we're just getting started."

He carried her to the bed. Griffin stripped her with hands that were tipped by claws, but he never so much as scratched her skin. His eyes gleamed. His face was savage. And then he was pulling her toward the edge of the bed, positioning her so that her hips were against the side of the mattress. He bent, kneeling, and then Griffin put his mouth on her sex.

Her eyes squeezed shut. She cried out his name as she arched toward him, so greedy for more of his lips and tongue. Her hands sank into his hair. Thick, soft hair. And his tongue slipped into *her.*

She almost forgot to breathe.

The things he could do with his mouth, the way he was licking her, the way he knew *exactly* where to touch her...Isabella was helpless. The second wave of release built within her, and there was no way to slow it down or stop it. She didn't want to stop it.

She didn't want to do anything but hold close to him.

But—but Griffin pulled back. He licked his lips and he stared at her as he rose to his full height beside the bed. "I'll be inside you this time. Feeling every fucking thing."

He lifted her legs, positioned her, and drove deep. He was thick and heavy and full, and she started climaxing, too far gone to slow down.

And he was leaning over her. He'd braced his arms on the bed as he thrust into her, long, wild strokes. His neck was so close to her mouth.

"Do it," Griffin growled.

She bit him as she came. As the pleasure flooded every cell of her body, Isabella sank her teeth into his neck. If possible, his cock grew even bigger inside of her. The pleasure seemed to deepen even more, and she was lost — absolutely lost in him.

He came inside of her, a hot surge of release. "*Isabella!*"

Her tongue licked over his neck, sealing the small puncture wounds she'd made. Her breath heaved out and her heart raced in her chest. Her legs were locked around his hips. Her nails had sunk into his broad shoulders. Pleasure still left her quaking.

His head lifted. His green eyes seemed to glow as he stared down at her.

She should have been afraid. She'd just gone from zero to implosion with a guy in less than five minutes. She should be pushing him back.

He smiled at her. "That was one hell of a start."

His dimple was sexy. He didn't look like some big, bad beast. He looked handsome. Charming. Like…like a lover. Her lover.

Because he was. A lover who hadn't been afraid when she'd bit him. She didn't need to use a compulsion to make him forget what she'd done. He'd liked her bite. He'd liked having sex with her. He'd just given her more pleasure than she could ever remember experiencing in her *very* long life.

But his smile slowly faded. His head turned, and he looked back at the door.

A chill skated over her body. "Griffin?"

He was still staring at the door. "Don't be afraid."

Um, she hadn't exactly been experiencing fear — not until that moment, anyway.

"I won't let them hurt you," he added grimly. "I swear it."

"Griff — "

The door flew inward, and Isabella screamed — it was an instinctive response to the fact that four freaking *wolves* had just rushed inside. Big, hulking beasts with saliva dripping from their bared fangs.

Griffin jumped to his feet — and she found a sheet tossed over her body in the same instance.

"Don't even fucking *think* about it," he snarled. He was completely naked, standing in front of her, blocking her from the wolves who'd just busted into their room. His claws were out, and she could see his shoulders heaving. "You won't touch her. She's *mine*."

Isabella scrambled off the bed and to her feet. She wrapped the sheet around her body and tried not to freak the hell out. The wolves had frozen in the doorway. She was surprised she didn't hear humans screaming outside. The motel was pretty much the pit of hell, but surely some mortal in the parking lot or in one of the rooms should have spotted the wolves?

The beast in front of the small pack—a particularly big, hulking wolf with thick, brown fur and glaring gold eyes—lunged forward. Griffin caught the beast and raked his claws over the animal's side. "Did you have trouble hearing what I said?" Griffin demanded. He tossed the brown wolf back.

The other beasts growled. The hair on Isabella's neck rose. This was so bad.

The brown wolf had hit the wall with a very solid thud. As Isabella watched, the beast began to change. Bones popped and reshaped. The fur melted from the wolf's body. Soon, a naked man was there. He rose, and she saw he was tall, thin...and still glaring with his golden eyes. "You're a dead wolf, Griffin."

Griffin just laughed. "Really? Because I feel oddly alive."

The three wolves at the door let out another chorus of growls.

"The alpha is waiting outside," the brown-haired fellow said. "You got one chance to save your ass before you face him."

Isabella's spine was ram-rod straight.

"Just how am I supposed to, um, save my ass?" Griffin asked, sounding only vaguely interested.

The brown-haired guy pointed at Isabella. "Kill the vamp bitch."

CHAPTER SIX

Kill the vamp bitch.

Griffin glanced around the dimly lit parking lot. It was full of werewolves—he'd smelled the pack coming. Sure, he'd been a bit distracted at the time, because he'd been balls deep in Isabella, but he'd realized he was being hunted.

He'd also decided he wasn't going to run. Running wasn't his style.

Isabella had been allowed to dress. She wore her sexy skirt, her tight top, and still no shoes. That fucking bothered him. He didn't want her feet hurt. She stood at his side, right in the middle of that circle of werewolves. At least most of the pack members were in human form, for the moment, anyway.

"Uh, Griffin?" A cough came from the left.

Griffin turned his head.

Carter rolled back his shoulders and looked highly uncomfortable. "I'm...I'm really sorry, man. But I did it to protect you."

Griffin lifted his brows.

"She's evil," Carter continued with a determined air. "You know the stories. You know what vamps will do—"

"Ah, excuse me," Isabella cut in. "But *she* is right here. And I'd really like to know what the hell is happening."

Griffin caught her hand in his. He brought her fingers to his mouth and kissed the back of her knuckles. He heard the snarls that came from the werewolves when he made that move. Screw them. Not like he really cared what they thought. Maybe once, he'd tried to follow the pack rules. But not now. Not any longer.

I've had her. She's mine. And I'll do anything to keep her.

Griffin kissed her knuckles once more. "I'm going to fight for you."

"Yes, but…*why?* I mean, don't get me wrong, I don't exactly want to be facing this pack alone but—*what is happening?*"

Carter locked his fingers around Griffin's shoulder. "You're digging your own grave, buddy. She's a parasite. A bloodsucker. She's not worth the pain you're going to take from the alpha."

Griffin let go of Isabella's fingers. She'd flinched at Carter's words—because those words had hurt her. Griffin gave Isabella a small smile, then he turned, and he drove his fist into Carter's face. His *ex*-friend slammed into the ground.

The snarls and growls around them stopped. Griffin threw back his shoulders and lifted his chin. "Good. I see I've got everyone's attention." He lifted his claws. He hadn't used his claws on Carter, but he *would* be using them on the next bastard who came at him or at Isabella. "I was told the alpha was waiting outside the motel room. Only now I'm outside, and I don't see him." He let his gaze drift around the crowd. "Is Vane hiding?" A deliberate taunt. A challenge.

"What in the hell are you doing?" Carter was on his feet and he'd rushed back to Griffin's side. "Just give up the vamp and you'll be okay. You don't need to get into some epic battle for her."

"Actually, I do, Carter. She's my mate."

Carter swore.

"And I'll fight to the death for her."

The color bleached from Carter's skin. "No…"

"Um, hello? *Again…I'm here.*" Isabella tapped Griffin's arm. "And I don't want you fighting to the death for me. Your death is the *last* thing I want."

That was cute. She cared, already. Definite progress. Griffin gave her a smile. "Sweetheart, I won't be the one dying." His death wouldn't protect her. Becoming the new alpha? That was the only way to keep her safe.

"Don't be too sure of that." The voice—loud, booming—was entirely too arrogant. Vane Bollen had finally shown himself. Tall, nearly six foot

three and with wide shoulders, the guy probably would have intimidated most people.

Not me.

Griffin had often wondered before who would win if he ever battled his alpha. When he'd come to town, Vane had been the wolf in charge, and Griffin hadn't cared enough to challenge the guy. Leadership wasn't exactly his bit. But...

He didn't have a choice any longer.

"Is it true?" Vane stalked forward, stopping when he was about five feet away from Griffin. "Did you mate the vamp bitch?"

"I don't like him," Isabella whispered to Griffin. "I think I want to punch his fat face."

"I'll take care of it," he promised her.

"*I* can fight my own battles."

A faint smirk curled Vane's thin lips. "She wants to challenge me?" He laughed. So did the others. At least fifteen werewolves were in that parking lot. No humans were around. They'd had the sense to clear out, probably because they thought a gang of bikers were riding into the area. That was what the werewolves there looked like—bikers wearing battered jeans and t-shirts. Lots of leather. With plenty of tats and bad fucking attitudes.

They were a pack, all right, just not the sort that the humans had first figured.

"Why not let the vamp have a go at me?" Vane smiled. "Let's see what she's got." His smile slipped away. "Before I tear her apart."

Isabella lunged forward, as if she'd go right at Vane, but Griffin held her back. He pulled her against his body, wrapping his arms around her so that her sweet little ass pressed to his cock. *Wrong time.*

"*Let me go,*" Isabella rasped.

He just held her tighter. He put his mouth to her ear. "It's a wolf thing. I have to kick Vane's ass because we are right in the middle of a pack challenge. You make a run at him, and all of the wolves will attack at once." And he couldn't fight off that many werewolves, not at one time. "I'm good, baby, but not that good." He could feel Carter watching them. Everyone was watching them. "But if I go against Vane on my own, if I challenge him for alpha status…" His breath blew over the shell of her ear. Isabella shivered. "Then I save us both."

"Or you kill both of you." Vane's mocking laughter echoed around them. Of course, the alpha would have heard Griffin's quiet words. Wolves could always hear nearly every damn thing. "Because you *won't* defeat me."

Griffin eased his hold on Isabella. She immediately spun in his arms and stared up at him. "He's going to attack you because of me. *I* should be the one fighting. I should—"

He kissed her and, damn, but she was sweet.

"*He's kissing the vamp!*" One werewolf shouted. "*She's making him weak! Kill her! Kill—*"

Griffin lifted his head. If he didn't take alpha status, the pack would swarm. "Hold the thought, Isabella. I'll be right back." He let her go. He'd put on jeans before he'd come into that parking lot, and he walked forward, clad in the jeans and nothing else.

"You sure you want to challenge me?" Vane stared at him. The alpha's arms were crossed over his chest. He wore jeans, boots, and a t-shirt. "In the last ten years, I've killed every werewolf who was dumb enough to come at me."

"You won't be killing me." Griffin had too much to live for.

Vane bounded forward, standing toe-to-toe with Griffin in an instant. "We aren't *pets* for the vampires," he hissed. "You would disgrace us all?"

"She's my mate." For a werewolf, there wasn't anything else to say. A mating was special. It was soul deep. With a bite, the beast could recognize his other half, long before the human part of Griffin realized what was happening. Nature's way of speeding up the process, hell, yes. The beast's way of saying...*I found the one who makes me whole.*

"You don't even know her." Vane sneered at him. "You think you're the first werewolf she went after? Not even close."

Griffin frowned. "What in the hell are you talking about?"

"Ask her." Vane nodded. "Ask her about the others. Because I heard of their deaths. Word reached me right before Carter came with his tale of you and your vamp." He lifted his hand and shoved his index finger into Griffin's chest. "Ask your pretty little vamp whore—"

Griffin caught that finger—and he broke it. One hard snap. "I'm asking you."

Vane hadn't made a sound when his finger broke. It took more than a little snap to hurt an alpha.

"I'm asking you," Griffin said again. "Tell me what in the hell you are talking about."

"I'm talking about the fact that your little vamp *killed* three other werewolves in her hunt to find a new…pet. Guess she got lucky with you, huh? Finally found the beast who would fucking bow to her."

Griffin glanced back at Isabella. She was staring at him with wide, dark eyes, her body tense, her—

Claws slashed across his stomach and a fist slammed into his jaw. *Sucker punch.* The werewolves around him started chanting. And it wasn't a fucking good chant.

"Death, death, death!"

"Death!"

Because the battle wouldn't end until either Vane was dead…or Griffin was. So Griffin clenched his teeth, and his claws slashed toward the alpha.

***

"Isabella is too valuable to lose." Felix stood inside of Griffin's office. His men had trashed the place, and they'd found *nothing*. They'd also searched every inch of Griffin's home, but they'd turned up nothing there, either. The bastard had vanished.

With my vampire.

His men kept searching. There was a thud as Griffin's computer hit the floor.

Where did you take Isabella?

"At least you know they're a match."

Felix's eyes snapped open. Bait was talking.

Bait. That was the nickname he'd given to the man he'd sent into the alley after Isabella during her ever-so-fateful first meeting with Griffin. But Bait had a real name, and it was Will Hasting. Will was sweating as he stood there. Will didn't like the paranormals—most of them scared the shit out of him. Well, with one small exception.

Will was a semi-intelligent guy, after all.

"I mean, Griffin didn't kill her in the alley. So if he has her now, you know he's protecting her. He'll keep her alive, and that gives us time to find them, right?" Will asked as he swiped a hand over his sweaty forehead.

"We're looking for a vampire and a werewolf. Two beings with enhanced strength and— as far as the wolf is concerned—very, very enhanced senses." The werewolf would hear them coming long before they got close to their target. "And if Isabella has any humans near her, she can use her compulsion on them. They'll give her aid." What a clusterfuck. "We should've had her at the hotel." He just hadn't counted on the woman flying out of the seventh floor window. Next time, he'd be better prepared. "We need to offer a bounty."

Will swallowed. "Like a dead or alive thing?"

"Isabella is no use to me dead." Why did everyone always assume a vamp was dead? A vamp's heart still beat, a vamp breathed air, a vamp needed blood to *live*. "I want her alive."

"R-right."

There were plenty of wolves in the city. Those wolves would be eager to kill a vampire, and he couldn't let that happen. No, no, he couldn't put a bounty on her head. Instead... "Put a bounty on him. Griffin Romeo. One hundred thousand dollars for information on his whereabouts." One hundred grand could tempt almost anyone. "Because wherever he is, our vamp will be close by."

Will didn't look convinced. "You sure about that? I mean, okay, even if their DNA made them some kind of mating bond...vamps and werewolves are mortal enemies."

Felix just laughed. "Not anymore, they're not. She's now his drug of choice, and he won't go anywhere without his fix."

***

"Wh-why haven't they shifted?" Isabella hated the stutter in her voice, but she was surrounded by a whole pack of werewolves, and she was scared. Actually, terrified would probably be a better word choice. Yet, strangely enough, the terror wasn't for herself.

It was for the bloody man who was fighting so viciously. *For Griffin.* Griffin had claw marks all over his body. Blood poured from him and from his opponent.

"They can't shift," Carter muttered. "That's against the rules." *Carter.* She'd heard Griffin say his name. Once the fighting had started, Carter had taken up a semi-protective position at her side. He didn't like her, though—none of those wolves did. *Only Griffin.* And if Griffin didn't kick the ass of the alpha, Isabella knew she was in serious trouble.

"What are the rules?" Isabella figured she should know them. Seemed important given the circumstances she was in.

As she watched the fight, the other wolf—*Vane? Yes, someone had shouted his name moments before* — plunged his claws into Griffin's stomach.

Isabella took a frantic step forward.

Carter grabbed her, his fingers biting into her arms. "Rule one…no interference. You try to help Griffin, and all of the other wolves will attack—they'll come for you *and* him."

Well, that was a crappy rule.

Griffin let out a hard roar. He punched Vane once, twice—a left hook, then a right. Vane staggered back. Griffin swiped out with his claws.

She bit her lip. All of that blood...vamps didn't do so well around *that* much blood. Her fangs were lengthening in her mouth. She could feel the slow burn in her gums.

"Rule two," Carter added as they watched the fight, "no shifting. You fight as a man, not as a beast because it's a control issue. If you want to be alpha, you have to prove that you can keep your beast in check. That the man is stronger than the monster."

She felt shock roll through her. "Griffin is fighting to be alpha?"

"No, I think he's fucking fighting for *you*." Disgust was rich in his voice. "He never cared about being alpha. He's doing this because it's the only way to keep the pack from ripping you to pieces."

Lovely visual.

"Vane is our alpha right now. And he's a tough sonofabitch, so this fight *won't* be easy."

Vane slipped and fell onto the parking lot pavement. Griffin immediately jumped on top of him. His claws went for Vane's throat, but the alpha blocked him. More blood spilled.

"Rule three...the fight doesn't stop until one man is dead."

Griffin drove his claws into Vane's chest. Right over his heart.

Vane let out a high, keening cry. His body arched upward, but then he fell back against the pavement.

Silence.

Griffin withdrew his claws. He knelt beside Vane a moment, his head bowed. Vane didn't appear to be breathing. And there was *so* much blood. Griffin rose. His breath came in heaving pants. He turned to face Isabella. His gaze held hers but…

His stare was hard. Cold. An icy fury radiated from the green depths of his eyes.

What did you expect? He just killed a man for you.

But Griffin was staring at her with such controlled and scary fury. He stalked toward her, moving with fast, angry strides despite all of the blood and—

"Behind you!" Isabella yelled.

Griffin whirled. Vane had lunged up from the ground. He charged at Griffin, his hand curled around a knife.

A knife? Why the hell would a werewolf need a knife? He has his own claws. He has —

In a move so fast her eyes could barely follow it, Griffin snatched the knife from Vane's hand— and then Griffin drove it deep into Vane's chest. Smoke immediately rose from the wound, mixing with the blood that soaked Vane's shirt.

"Silver," Carter spat in disgust. "That damn asshole had a silver knife hidden on him. That's cheating."

Smoke was still rising from Vane's chest. Isabella was afraid to take her eyes off him. What if he got up again and attacked? What if he just kept coming? What—

"She broke the rules!" A male voice shouted. "The vamp interfered!"

Snarls and growls followed that shout and suddenly, a whole lot of angry werewolves were moving toward her. Closing in.

Carter stepped fully in front of her. "Vane was using a *silver* knife. I saw it in his hand. He broke the rules before she said a word. The victory *stands*."

He'd barely uttered that final word before he was shoved to the side—by Griffin. Griffin's big, angry, *bloody* self was suddenly right in front of Isabella. She stared up at him a moment, absolutely certain her heart had stopped. He glared. She—she threw her arms around him.

"You scared the life out of me," Isabella muttered, holding him tight. He was as stiff as a statue in her arms, making no move to hold her in return. Embarrassed, Isabella pulled back. The scent of his blood was so strong. It nearly overwhelmed her. Her teeth were fully extended, and she knew all of the werewolves had to see them.

Griffin has so many wounds. He's bleeding too much.

She pushed her wrist toward his mouth. "Here. Take my blood. It will help you heal faster."

"Werewolves heal plenty fast on their own," Carter told her, rather arrogantly. "They—"

Griffin bit her. She gave a little gasp and her body went from petrified to *alive.* Pulsing. Throbbing. Aching.

That bite of his held a definite kick.

The werewolves stopped muttering. Everyone just went dead silent.

As he bit her, Griffin's gaze stayed on her. His mouth was on her wrist, and she *knew* he'd bit her in the exact same spot as before. She could feel it. As if his brand had been placed on her again.

Mates? Was that really possible?

"What the fuck are we supposed to do now?"

Her head jerked at those low words. She wasn't even sure which werewolf had asked that growly question.

Griffin's tongue swiped over her wrist. It was an oddly tender move, especially considering that they were standing in the middle of a raving wolf pack.

"Now..." Griffin's voice carried easily. "You pick up the dead. We bury him." That cold gaze of his never left her face. "And I find out just what fucking secrets this vamp has been keeping from me."

Her jaw dropped in shock.

And the werewolves howled...as if...as if in victory.

It was right then that Isabella realized she was still in some serious shit.

CHAPTER SEVEN

The water pounded down on Griffin's body, washing away the blood, but doing damn little to cool his fury—even though the water was ice cold.

He'd killed the alpha. He was now the leader of the toughest werewolf pack on the West Coast. The wolves were going to bow to him...

And he didn't care.

Did she lie to me? Is she a cold-blooded killer?

He yanked at the faucet, turning it off with a hard flick of his wrist. He left the shower, barely pausing to dry off before he wrapped the towel around his hips. Then he was storming back through the bedroom—the bedroom of his new house. Turned out that being the alpha came with all kinds of perks, and one of those perks was the sweet-ass mansion that was now his home. One hidden in the desert, back from the bright lights of Vegas. A place that promised him a life of luxury.

If you were into that kind of thing.

He stormed into the hallway and nearly rammed right into Carter. "Where is she?" Griffin immediately demanded. He'd taken the shower to try and calm the hell down before he questioned Isabella. And because he hadn't wanted to touch her with so much blood on him. He figured he'd probably looked like some freaking four-course meal covered in all that blood. A real feast for a vamp. But…

She hadn't bitten him. She'd exercised what had to be supreme vampire control. He'd seen her little fangs, so he'd known Isabella was tempted. *Why the hell do I find those small fangs sexy?* Only instead of sinking her fangs into him, Isabella had given him her blood.

Because she cared? Or because she was playing a game? Tricking him?

"Uh…you want to put some clothes on first?" Carter asked, raising his brows.

"Since when do werewolves care about modesty?" He was fine in the towel. "Where. Is. She?"

"I sent guards with her and put her in the guest room in the west wing." Carter pointed down the hallway.

The place had wings? Holy hell. If he'd known Vane was sitting on this much cash, Griffin might have challenged the prick sooner. Vane had always enjoyed the bloodshed a bit too much, but the old alpha hadn't liked getting his hands dirty. He'd preferred to watch the violence and battles from a distance.

That was where I came in. I did the dirty work for him. Griffin had done the cleaning up for years, taking care of the pack's secrets ever since he'd come to Vegas. Griffin had grown up in one of the most brutal packs in the world. His parents had been dead before he'd been ten, and he'd bounced around from pack family to pack family, never truly feeling as if he belonged. At eighteen, he'd set out on his own. He'd made a living by doing anything necessary, and then he'd finally wound up in Vegas.

He'd liked the bright lights, liked the rush of the city, so he'd decided to stay. He and Vane had formed a truce, of sorts, and life had just gone right along.

Until I had to end Vane's life.

But right before Griffin had sent Vane to the afterlife, another secret had been spilled.

She's done this before. She killed three other werewolves. Vane's words kept echoing in Griffin's head.

"Don't worry," Carter assured him. "The guards aren't going to let her walk away. She's showering, just like you were."

"She'll need fresh clothes."

A deep furrow appeared between Carter's brows. "Didn't you just say that werewolves didn't care about modesty?"

His hand fisted on Carter's shirt-front. "She's a vamp, not a werewolf. And she's *mine*." Even if she was a cold-blooded killer, she still belonged to him. "I don't want the rest of the pack seeing her naked." If they saw her body, he'd pretty much have to kill them all.

Carter gulped. "Right. We'll get her clothes right away. Something big and loose—totally covering."

Griffin let him go.

But instead of retreating, Carter stood his ground. "I was trying to protect you."

At those words, Griffin laughed.

Carter flushed. "We've all heard the stories about vampires. I didn't want her to destroy you."

The way she'd destroyed three other wolves?

"Is it…true?" Now Carter was hesitant. "Did you feel the bond click into place between you?"

"The bond is there." He headed down the hallway. He needed to see Isabella. Needed to touch her. Needed to get the truth from her.

Carter followed on his heels. "What does it feel like? I mean, I've only met werewolves with the bond. I've never witnessed someone with a vamp—"

Griffin stilled. He could see the werewolves who guarded the west wing. They shifted nervously in front of the closed bedroom door. "It feels like I found the other half of my soul. I want her more than I want breath, and I'll destroy anyone who hurts her."

"Yeah, that's intense."

You have no idea. "Vane said she killed three werewolves."

"What?"

Griffin's head turned. He pinned Carter with a hard glare. "I want to know if that's true. Spread word to the other packs. See if any werewolves have been murdered recently, and, if so, I want to know exactly *how* they died."

Carter nodded and immediately rushed down the hallway. Griffin squared his shoulders and marched toward the bedroom—and the guards. "I've got her now," he said to the werewolves.

They lowered their heads, didn't speak, and hurried away. His hand lifted and his fingers curled around the doorknob. He twisted the knob and a moment later, the door was opening soundlessly. He walked into the bedroom. The thick carpeting swallowed the sound of his steps.

The bedroom was empty. A big, four-poster bed waited to the right. A cherry-wood dresser was to the left. And Isabella—

She opened the bathroom door. Steam drifted out of the bathroom and floated lazily in the air around her. Her wet hair trailed over her bare shoulders, and a thick, white towel was wrapped around her body.

"Griffin." His name carried both relief and fear as it broke from her lips. "I was wondering when I'd see you again."

He closed the bedroom door behind him. For a minute, he just stood there, staring at her. Beautiful Isabella.

Lying Isabella?

He leaned back, and his shoulders pressed to the wood of the door. "Did you kill them?"

She took a step forward. "I...I told you about my past already. It wasn't pretty, and I'm *not* proud of the things I did. I've tried to be better. I left my family and the vampire friends I had — they wanted me to stay on their path, but I needed to change, I needed—"

"No." His voice was cold and flat, and Griffin was surprised by that fact. Fury pumped through him, so he'd expected more fire from himself.

Isabella licked her lower lip. "No—what, exactly?"

"Did you kill the werewolves?"

Her eyes widened. She crept closer to him, then, whispering, she asked, "What werewolves?"

His jaw clenched. *Don't lie to me, Isabella.*

She advanced with hesitant steps. "What werewolves are you talking about?" But then, before he could speak, she gave a nervous laugh. "Doesn't matter, though, not really, because I've never killed a werewolf. You were actually the first werewolf I ever saw. You know, up close and in the flesh."

Her words sounded like the truth.

But...

Vampires and werewolves didn't exactly have the best past. "Vane said you'd tried to mate with others." The bastard had still been whispering his secrets even as Griffin shoved the silver knife into the guy's heart. Vane had told him, "*She was working her way through the wolves, killing those who didn't form a link with her. It's what her kind does…*"

She put her hand on his chest. "I was scared." Her long lashes covered her eyes as she made that soft confession. "I know it's crazy. I just met you. I feel like everything is moving a million miles an hour between us, but…I was scared when you were fighting. I didn't like seeing you hurt, and I did *not* want you to die in front of me." Her lashes lifted. "I would have broken every single one of those stupid werewolf rules to keep you alive."

Could she really lie that well? Or was he just desperate to believe her? "We have the mating link. Nothing can destroy that."

"I…um, that's good to know."

"So even if I found out that you've been killing werewolves, the link would still be there."

She blinked.

"Even if I found out that I was just number four in your line—that you'd planned to kill me, too, if the mating bond didn't form between us— our *link* would still be there."

Isabella snatched her hand away from his chest. "I don't think I like the way you're looking at me."

Too bad. He didn't much like the way he was feeling. Since meeting Isabella, his emotions had erupted. Right then, he was feeling rage, fear, lust...and jealousy. The jealousy didn't even make sense. But...*three other werewolves before me?* That thought just opened the doors and made him wonder...who all had she known before him? What lovers had tasted Isabella?

"I don't like the way you're talking to me, either." Her chin notched up. "You know, I saved your ass out there. Vane was charging right at you. I didn't hear your buddy Carter warning you about the attack. *I* did that. And you still haven't offered me even a grudging thank you."

"I've got werewolf's senses," he responded flatly. "I heard Vane coming. I didn't need your shout." But it had been nice.

Her lips tightened.

He wanted those lips. He wanted her. But Griffin wasn't sure he could trust her. "Felix said you were a killer."

"Felix?" Isabella backed up a step. "Please...seriously, tell me you aren't talking about an asshole named Felix Flemming."

She knew the name, obviously. Not a good sign. "I'm talking about the asshole in question."

Isabella swallowed. "He...he was the guy who came to my hotel room in Vegas. He and his goons tried to force me to go with them. I didn't particularly appreciate a creep with a gun trying to abduct me, so I jumped out of the window."

He surged forward and curled his fingers around her arms. "Felix is the reason you jumped from the seventh story?"

"Are *you* working with Felix?"

Griffin hesitated. Horror was on her pretty face and admitting that he'd taken cash from Felix didn't seem like the best plan at that moment. "Tell me everything Felix said in your hotel room."

"He said that he'd been waiting on me for a very long time." She gave a mocking laugh. "I'm a vamp. The guy doesn't understand the meaning of *long time*."

"What *else* did he say?"

She licked her lower lip, a fast and sexy swipe of her tongue. His cock jerked beneath the towel. "Felix told me that the, ah, the first experiments were failures, but that he had high hopes…" She shook her head. "I can't remember if he said high hopes about *me* or high hopes about *that night* because that's the point when he started saying that he knew my weakness. The guy threatened to shoot me so that I'd be weakened from blood loss. Once I was weak, he was going to get his jerk henchmen to take me out of the hotel."

Sonofabitch. "He's a dead man."

"How do *you* know Felix?"

Because he hired me to hunt you. "Our paths have crossed."

"How." But her eyes narrowed as she studied him. Anger flashed on her face. "Right. I get it. The stake in the alley…he sent you to kill me."

Griffin knew he needed to explain *very* carefully. "Felix sent me after a *killer*. He told me you were a threat, that you'd been attacking humans. The guy came into my office and said he just wanted proof of your guilt." But Griffin could see the lies now. "Felix knew what I was," Griffin realized. "He must have known. He deliberately sent a werewolf after a vamp, knowing what would happen when our paths crossed."

"My death. That was supposed to happen. You were supposed to drive your stake into my heart."

That was one option. "Or maybe he got exactly what he really wanted." *High fucking hopes, indeed.* "If there are other dead werewolves out there, those could be the failed experiments. The ones who didn't form the mating link with you."

She glared at him. "I *told* you, I hadn't met any werewolves until you! I never saw any others *until you!*"

That didn't mean the werewolves hadn't seen her. He was still holding her. Beneath his fingers, her skin was softer than silk. He loved touching her skin. Kissing it. Kissing her everywhere. "We'll get to the bottom of this."

"Don't."

He blinked.

"Don't you dare look at me like you want to fuck me now. Not after you stood in that horrible parking lot with a dead wolf at your feet, and you stared at me as if *I* were the monster."

"Isabella…"

"You thought I'd lied. I mean, I get it now. I *see* now. You thought I'd been picking off werewolves—"

"It was something I had to consider, especially since Vane had just told me you were guilty."

Her lips parted. "He told you that…and you…still killed him? For me?"

"I said it before, and I'll say it again, no one will threaten you." Because when he thought about her in danger, Griffin went a little mad. More than a little. "My feelings for you aren't exactly normal."

Her tongue swiped over her lower lip. She needed to stop doing that—unless she was going to let him lick, too.

Her voice was breathy as Isabella said, "You think mine are normal when it comes to you? I'm mad as hell at you right now." Her voice dropped even more. "But the desire is still there. The need—it's twisting and growing inside of me, and I know it's wrong."

His mouth took hers. A long, drugging kiss, and his cock hardened even more for her. "Nothing between us will ever be wrong." Screw what the other werewolves thought of their union. Fate had different plans for him. With the mating bond, the lust came first—the instant connection that said two parts of a whole had found each other. Love? Trust? He knew they would come soon enough.

Hell, they'd already started growing for him. Wasn't he taking Isabella at her word, even over a werewolf alpha? Hadn't he been so frantic to protect her that he'd gone against his entire pack?

But how did she feel about him?

"Don't be so sure of that," she told him. Her eyes gleamed and he was pretty sure those eyes of hers were stealing part of his soul. "The entire situation feels wrong."

He kissed her again. "Then let's make it feel right." His hand slid between their bodies. She'd secured the towel between her breasts, and he tugged on the material. The towel fell and pooled at her feet.

"Griffin..."

"You let me bite you at the motel." When he'd been bleeding and hurt, she'd come to his aid. "I think it's your turn." His fingers lightly caressed her nipples. Such pretty, tight nipples. A soft, dusky color.

She shivered. "I think the bites...they make things worse." Her head tipped back and her eyes closed as his fingers stroked her. "They just make me want you more."

That's not worse. It's better.

"You thought I was a killer just moments before, and now you want to fuck me?"

He lifted her up, holding her easily in his arms. "Isabella, let's get one thing straight. I *always* want to fuck you."

Her eyes opened as a surprised laugh tumbled out of her. He'd been carrying her toward the bed, but at that sound, he froze.

The entire world seemed to stop.

She blinked. "What is it?" Isabella stiffened in his arms. "Is something the matter?"

He wanted to hear her laughter again. He wanted to see her smile. He wanted her happy.

That was the way of the bite. Lust came first, the instant connection and consuming need. And then…

Love? Did he truly believe in love?

I think I could believe in her. Griffin cleared his throat. "I like your laugh."

Carefully, he lowered her onto the bed. Griffin wasn't particularly shocked to see that he'd lost his own control. Not shocked — and he didn't care, either. She was spread out on the bed, completely open to his gaze, and he'd never seen anything so perfect in his life.

He leaned over her, and his mouth closed over one sweet nipple. He licked her, sucked, and loved the way she arched toward him. Did Isabella know she was whispering his name? Did she have any clue how much her whisper turned him on?

His hand slipped between her legs. One touch, and he found that she was ready for him. Wet and hot. A good thing because his cock was stretched to the brink. He wanted *in* her. He wanted her pleasure. He wanted to watch her come.

And he wanted her bite. Because he liked that, too. Griffin didn't care if the bite made the link between them stronger. Hell, he *wanted* it stronger. *I won't let her go.*

He would also never forget the way she'd come to him in that parking lot...surrounded by a pack of angry wolves, offering her blood to his beast.

Now he offered himself to her. *The trust has to start somewhere. It can start with me.* He kissed a path down her stomach, loving the moans and gasps that slid from her lips. Down, down he went. His fingers trailed over her sex. He'd never witnessed a prettier sight.

His head bent. His lips feathered over her.

"Griffin!"

His tongue slipped into her.

"Griffin!" Her whole body shuddered. Then her hands grabbed for his shoulders. "I want you, *all* of you, *in me.*"

As if he'd deny her. A moment later, Griffin drove into her. Slid right into the tightest, hottest heaven of his life. Her legs wrapped around his hips as she surged up to meet his thrusts. The headboard slammed into the wall, but he didn't care. She was all that mattered.

They rolled on the bed, and then she was on top. Her hands pushed against his chest as she rose up and sank down. Her head tipped back, her dark hair trailing over her shoulders. Her breath came quickly, and she rode him faster, faster.

He surged upward, his thrust lifting her off the bed. She came that way, gasping out his name, but it wasn't enough for him. Not nearly enough. "Bite me."

She slumped forward. Her mouth pressed to his throat. Isabella licked the skin right over his racing pulse. His fingers dug into her hips as he drove into her again. His climax was bearing down on him, but he needed—

Her fangs sank into him.

The whole world shattered. Pleasure was all he knew.

***

"Word on the street…word is that the Vegas pack has a new leader."

Felix stared at the fire before him—the fire that blazed inside the piece of shit office that had once been the home of Romeo Private Investigations. After he'd finished searching the dump, Felix had thought the fire would be a nice touch.

The flames would destroy any evidence he'd left behind, and the blaze might even draw Griffin back to the city. In the distance, Felix could hear the wail of sirens. Cops, firefighters — rushing to the blaze. If they were coming, then Felix knew it was time for him to make an exit.

"Did you hear me, boss?" Will Hasting demanded.

"I heard you." He kept looking at the flames. The fire was such a greedy bitch, destroying everything in her path. She was a thing of utter beauty to him. "Who took over?"

"Don't know yet. When I put out the call for intel on Griffin, I immediately learned from my main source that Vane was dead."

"Your source." His lips twisted. "You mean your werewolf side piece." Because the guy liked to walk — or fuck — on the wild side with one of the female wolves in the pack. She'd been the one feeding them information about the pack from day one. Felix had learned — early on — that every pack had a weakness. That weakness was typically the runt of the litter. A wolf the others treated like shit. In the case of the Vegas pack, Shelly Crenshaw was the runt. She couldn't shift fully, and she'd been scorned for years because of that fact. Trapped between life as a human and life as a werewolf, Shelly had been utterly alone and the perfect prey.

Will had moved in on her, seduced her, and gotten her to spill pack secrets in near record time. As for Felix...*I learned plenty of secrets about Shelly, too.* Secrets that had proved useful to him.

"Shelly doesn't know who the new alpha is. She wasn't at the fight."

Of course, she hadn't been. Shelly wouldn't have been included in something so important.

"But she heard Vane's body was being buried." Will whistled. "Vane's death has to be connected to Griffin, right? I mean, hell, do you think *he* challenged Vane?"

It was a possibility that couldn't be overlooked. "If Vane found out that Griffin was mated to a vamp, then the fight would have been inevitable." Vane would have wanted to kill Isabella, and Griffin would now be hard-wired to protect her at all costs. *My experiment just gets better and better.*

The sirens were coming closer. Felix turned from the scene and stalked toward the black SUV that waited for him. He climbed inside, and Will hurried in after him. Felix's driver slammed the back door shut. As he sat in the back seat, Felix tapped his chin. "Pack law..." He'd made a point of learning everything he could about pack law over the years. *Know your enemy.* "Whoever defeated Vane now gets everything the old alpha possessed."

Will leaned back against the leather seat. "Sounds like one sweet ass deal to me."

It was. *Provided you survived the fight to the death.* "Vane's house." A slow smile spread over his lips. "Griffin would have won Vane's house." He already knew all about that place, courtesy of the chatty Shelly. A big, fancy mansion in the desert. The perfect place for the pack to run wild. "That's where Griffin is right now. The guy went from that piece of shit office..." Ah, but it was burning so well. "To paradise. He's going to be in the mansion." Felix laughed. "And he'll have my vamp with him." *Found out all this...and didn't even have to pay the hundred grand.*

The driver slid into the front seat. "Where to, boss?"

Felix peered through the window, staring up at the dark sky. He wouldn't attack, not until dawn. But he could go ahead and make his plans.

You can run, Isabella, but you can't hide. Not from me.

CHAPTER EIGHT

Sex wasn't supposed to be so consuming. An orgasm wasn't supposed to practically shatter her, and when Isabella bit her donor, his blood wasn't supposed to make her entire body *hum* with pleasure.

But Griffin wasn't just some donor. And sex with him would never be considered average or casual. And the orgasms he gave to her? *More, please.*

She was in bed with him. The sheets felt cool against her skin, but his arm was warm as it wrapped around her stomach. Her heart was still racing, she swore she could still feel him, inside, and Isabella knew she was in serious trouble.

She stared up at the ceiling. "Lust comes first."

He pressed a kiss to her shoulder.

Her eyes closed. "Then…love?" Was that really the way it worked? Was it even possible? The bite recognized physical compatibility, okay, she could go with that, but…

"You ever been in love before, Isabella?"

"No." Not even close. "Vamps aren't exactly, well, long-term commitment isn't possible, not with a human lover." A lover who would die and leave you alone and grieving. "And other vamps…" Okay, time for her confession. "I don't exactly have the best relationship with my own kind." Her eyes opened. Her head turned. She found his gaze on her. "I've been running," she admitted, her voice stark.

"Tell me who you want me to kill."

Her lips parted in shock. "What?"

"If someone's after you, tell me. Give me a name. Or names. I don't care if it's one vamp or an army of them, I will—"

"I left them because I didn't want to—I didn't want to live that way, not anymore."

"What way?"

It was so hard to tell him about the dark places inside of her. "The bloodlust can overtake you. You forget that you have a soul. You're just feeding and getting high on the rush of power and life. Nothing else matters. And then you look down and you realize…the blood is all around you, and there's…there's a body on the floor."

His face hardened.

"I don't like to kill." Her words came out in a rush. "I don't want to take and take until nothing is left. I learned control. I *made* myself learn it. But the others, they didn't care. They said I was unnatural. That we were the top of the food chain, and we could do what we wanted."

"Isabella…"

"I've made plenty of mistakes. I've hurt people, and I can't ever forget what I did to them, but I am trying, I swear, *I am trying*, to be better. That's why I only attack people who deserve it."

His gaze didn't leave her face.

She felt shame burn through her. Isabella rolled away from him and crawled from the bed. "You think no one deserves what I do. That I shouldn't bite any human."

"Isabella…"

She grabbed a towel that she found on the floor and wrapped it around her body. "The man in the alley—he wanted to hurt me. So I picked him as a donor." *Donor is the wrong word. He didn't volunteer. No one ever volunteers. I take and I take, and…*

I kill.

Her hand lifted and pressed to her mouth. She covered her fangs.

Griffin sat up in bed. "You go after bastards."

Her hand fell back to her side. She couldn't hide what she was. Not from him. "I go after predators. The ones who think they are so big and bad, hunting in the night. I hunt *them*." Her shoulders straightened. "But I don't kill them. I stop myself. And I leave them with a compulsion. To not hurt another innocent. To change."

He rose and walked toward her. His steps were slow and certain.

"I never asked to be what I am," Isabella said.

His hand lifted and the back of his knuckles stroked over her cheek. "I rather like what you are."

She swallowed the lump that rose in her throat. "You wouldn't have liked me, if you knew me before." A century ago, he would have hated her.

"Don't be too sure of that."

"My very name—Abandonato—it means forsaken. That's what I am. What my family is." Isabella's lips parted. "Griffin, I—"

A knock sounded at the door. Griffin whirled to face the door, putting his body in front of hers. "Who is it?"

The door cracked open. Isabella peered around Griffin's side and saw Carter poke his head inside the room. "Three are dead."

Her heart lurched.

"Three werewolves." Carter wasn't looking at her. His attention was on Griffin. "The first was killed in New York three weeks ago."

A knot formed in Isabella's stomach. Three weeks ago, she'd been in New York.

"One was killed in Washington, D.C., the next week."

She rocked back on her heels. *D.C. was my next stop.*

"Then a wolf was found dead in Aspen six days ago."

Her eyes squeezed shut. *This can't be happening.*

"How did they die?" Griffin's voice was cold. Flat.

"They were found with puncture wounds on their necks…and silver bullets in their hearts."

"No!" The sharp denial broke from Isabella even as her eyes flew open. Carter was looking at her then, and so was Griffin. Griffin had turned so that his intense green gaze fell on her.

"I didn't do this!" Isabella needed Griffin to believe her. "I was in those places." Why not go ahead and admit that? He'd find out. It seemed as if the guy had a whole werewolf network at his fingertips now that he was alpha. "But I did not kill them, I swear it. I didn't even meet them! I told you that before!"

Silence.

"You…believe me, don't you?" He had to believe her.

His gaze glinted. "We need to find fucking Felix."

Griffin's words had been a growl. They hadn't been the hard, fast vow of *I absolutely believe you, yes!* But…they were better than nothing.

Then Griffin reached for her hand. His fingers curled around her wrist, going right to the spot where he'd bit her — twice. The spot that still felt like a brand to her. "Felix wanted me to hunt you. He sent me on a path to collide with you. He knew I was a werewolf. And if a werewolf found a vamp hunting, if a werewolf saw a vamp drinking from a human, the wolf's first instinct would be to kill."

Her eyes widened. "That's why you came at me with your stake."

Carter cleared his throat. "Uh, you tried to stake her? You didn't mention that part to me."

Griffin didn't look away from her. "The bond was between us. I *couldn't* hurt you."

"When you first put the stake to my heart, the bite hadn't occurred."

His voice lowered as he said, "Maybe part of me already knew…"

Her heart was racing too fast, and she'd put the puzzle pieces together. "You were number four."

Griffin nodded. "I think I was."

"Felix set me up over and over, didn't he?" And that thought was terrifying.

"Uh, who the hell is Felix?" Carter demanded.

Isabella kept talking. "The other three werewolves…"

"I think he sent them after you, too." Griffin's expression could have been carved from stone. "Only they weren't showing any signs of bonding with you. There was no connection. They were going to kill you —"

"But I never even saw them! Wouldn't we have needed the bite, at least? I mean, how else would we even know if the bonding was going to work?"

"The first three werewolves didn't make it to that step. I *felt* something inside of me reacting to you. From the first moment I saw you in that alley, I was pulled to you. Even as I held that stake, I knew I couldn't hurt you. The connection was there before the bite. Taking your blood, giving you mine—that just sealed the deal."

The drumming of her heartbeat seemed to echo in her ears. "The others didn't feel any connection." That was what he was saying. "They saw me...p-probably feeding." Because she'd had to feed to survive. "And they were going to attack me."

Carter sauntered toward them. "Only they were the ones to die." He grimaced. "Sorry, just following along with what you two are saying. If the other werewolves were part of some damn test, then if they weren't passing the test, they'd be eliminated. I mean...hell, we all know there are more werewolves than vamps in the world. You guys don't exactly reproduce a lot."

No, they didn't. Because despite the Hollywood hype, it wasn't easy to transform a human into a vampire. Usually, the transformation just resulted in a permanent death and not in an undead life.

Griffin's fingers slid over her wrist in a light caress. "Isabella is even more precious than you realize. She was born as a vamp."

"Seriously? Shit, that's a new one."

Her head whipped toward Carter. He was eyeing her as if she were some kind of lab rat.

"Never seen a born before," he added as the guy practically gawked at her.

Her shoulders straightened. "And I'd never seen a werewolf, not until Griffin."

Carter laughed. "And your first turned out to be your mate. What are the odds?"

But Griffin wasn't laughing. "I was number four, not number one. Three other werewolves died before me." Then he let go of Isabella. "Fucking hell. He was watching."

Isabella didn't move.

"The bastard had to have eyes on us in that alley. He was watching to see what I'd do when I got near you."

Carter cleared his throat. "Uh, yeah, *alpha*, nice idea, but that's total bullshit. You have enhanced senses—don't you think you would have noticed if someone was hanging around and spying on you?"

"I was so lost in her that I probably wouldn't have noticed a damn thing." The admission was gruff. "And maybe that's the difference between me and the others. Maybe they weren't so tuned to her, and those werewolves realized they were being tailed by Felix and his men. Those werewolves confronted Felix—and they died."

Yes, that sounded like one option, but he was overlooking one important fact. "Puncture wounds."

Griffin frowned.

"The bodies had puncture wounds on their throats." She gave a sad shake of her head. "Only a vamp would do that."

Griffin seemed to consider what she'd said. "Then maybe Felix has a vamp on his side."

Before she could respond, there was another hard knock on the door. Carter had shut it when he entered the room, and now someone else was out there, pounding so fiercely that Isabella knew their little group was about to get more bad news.

Griffin strode forward and yanked open the door.

A young werewolf was there—and he was sweating. "Alpha...we just...we just got news about your PI office..."

"What? What the hell news did you get?"

The guy's Adam's apple bobbed and sweat trickled down the side of his face. He truly looked as if he wished he were *anywhere* else. "It's burning, alpha. The place is burning to the ground."

CHAPTER NINE

"You *cannot* be serious." Isabella glared at Griffin.

Did the woman have any idea just how sexy she was when she glared? Probably not. And Griffin didn't think this was the best time to clue her in to that fact.

"You are going to leave me in a den of werewolves?"

"It's the safest place for you."

Her jaw dropped. *"In a den of werewolves? How is that possibly safe?"*

His fingers curled under her chin. "I'm alpha. You're my mate. No one here would *dare* hurt you. They'd give their very lives to protect you."

"That's bullshit. They won't save a vampire."

"That's werewolf law. Their job is to protect the alpha's mate. Always." He pressed a kiss to her lips. A mistake because when he tasted her, he wanted more. "Why do you think I became alpha?" he rasped against her soft mouth. "To protect *you*." Griffin made himself step away from her. He had a job to do—and a bastard to hunt down. "Dawn will come soon. I can't risk

having you out in the open when you do your vamp thing."

Her eyes glittered. "My vamp thing?"

"Yeah, you know what I'm talking about." They were alone in the bedroom. "When daylight hits, you'll be dead to the world."

"I will *not* be dead! Vampires aren't dead! We're *undead*."

He stared at her. "My bad. You'll be sleeping very heavily."

She blew out a hard breath. "I'll be weak. *That's* what you mean."

"And as your mate, it's my job to protect you when you're weak. I'll leave werewolf guards here. *No one* will get to you. You rest and by the time you open your eyes, I'll have Felix." That was a grim promise. "No one hunts better than a werewolf. The bastard will pay for his crimes."

She turned from him and paced away from the bed. The windows had already been covered with heavy draperies, by Griffin's request. She paused in front of one of those windows, her shoulders stiff. "What if he has a vampire working with him? What if we're right about that part?"

"All the more reason for me to hunt during the day."

"The vamp's weakest point," she said, not glancing back at him.

"Yes."

"I hate having this weakness." And he could hear the frustration in her voice. "I want to help you."

You have, sweetheart, and you don't even realize how much. You've changed my world.

She spun to face him, her hands going to her hips. "You'd better come back without so much as a scratch on you, do you understand? Because if you get hurt, I will be pissed."

He laughed, the sound erupting and catching him off guard.

"I am *serious*."

His laughter faded. "Careful, Isabella, or you'll make me think you care."

Her chin notched up the smallest bit. "That's the problem, wolf. I think I do. I don't understand how things happened this fast, but... *I do.* And I don't want anything happening to you, so bring that furry butt of yours back to me, got it? You also need to promise to let me have a run at Felix. He's been playing with my life, and I want to know why."

Griffin couldn't promise to keep the bastard alive, not when Felix had been targeting Isabella, so he just gave her one last smile and turned for the door.

"Your real smile shows your dimple."

He stilled.

"It flashes every now and then. I saw it when you laughed."

Griffin glanced over his shoulder.

"I like the real smile." She gave him a small smile of her own. "I like the real you."

Could you ever love the real me?

Lust comes first…then love?

"Come back to me — without a scratch."

"I will." And he hoped like hell that he wouldn't have to break that promise.

***

She didn't like staying behind. An hour had passed since Griffin had left her. Isabella could feel the power of the rising sun. Lethargy had swept over her. Her body felt sluggish and heavy, and she *hated* that feeling. She wanted to be with Griffin. Hunting.

Not sleeping.

Clothes had been brought to her. Jeans that fit like a glove, a loose t-shirt. Shoes. Even a bra and a pair of silk panties. They'd all come courtesy of Griffin.

The guy was looking out for her, and he was getting beneath her skin. *And into my heart?*

The door to her bedroom swung open. Isabella turned to find a young, red-haired woman just…walking right into her room.

The woman drew up short when she saw Isabella. "Oh! Sorry! I thought you'd already be asleep."

"What?"

The redhead glanced over her shoulder, seemingly nervous. "I'm not supposed to be here."

"Right...it's probably a bad idea to waltz into someone's bedroom unannounced."

The woman edged closer. "I'm Shelly."

"And I'm—"

"The vampire," Shelly said dramatically as her gaze swept over Isabella.

Isabella lifted a brow. She was freaking exhausted. Standing up was an effort, and now the redhead in front of her was staring at Isabella as if she were a freak. So much for that promised werewolf protection.

"I had to see you for myself," Shelly added as her eyes flared wide. "What's it like?" She crept even closer to Isabella. "I mean, I couldn't believe it when I heard that you were the new alpha's mate. A *vampire.* I thought the wolves hated anyone who wasn't a perfect predator like they were." There was a strange mix of pain and disgust in her voice as she said those words.

Isabella tried to focus on the small werewolf. Well, she'd assumed the woman was a werewolf. Now that she knew Griffin, Carter, and a few of the others, Isabella had realized that werewolves tended to carry a wild, woodsy scent. That scent was missing from the woman before her. "What are you?"

Shelly flinched. "Million dollar question."

One that the woman hadn't answered.

Shelly clenched her hands into fists. "Can you turn me?"

What? Shelly was about five foot four inches tall, and built along small, delicate lines. Her face had a pale, almost otherworldly beauty. And she just looked *fragile.* Hardly fierce werewolf material.

And the chick just asked to be turned.

"Werewolves can't be turned." The words slipped from Isabella. "That's what I've always heard, and Griffin told me the same thing recently."

Anger flashed on Shelly's face. "Just because you've always heard something…doesn't make it true."

Isabella's knees wanted to buckle. *The sun is rising.* "I—"

"Shelly!"

Carter was in the doorway, glowering. He marched into the bedroom. "What in the hell are you doing in here? How'd you get past the guards?"

Shelly just laughed, but it was a sad sound. "I don't think they even noticed me. No one in the pack ever does."

Carter's face hardened. "Shelly, you need to leave, *now.*"

"Story of my life. I just wanted to see the vampire for myself."

Carter curled his hand around her arm and led her to the door. "Alpha's orders. Isabella isn't to be disturbed today."

"Because she matters." Shelly glanced back at her. "The mate."

"*Shelly...*" A warning edge cut in his voice.

"I'm gone. Don't worry, it will be like I was never even here." Shelly laughed. "Isn't it always?" She walked slowly from the room.

Isabella grabbed the edge of the bed. She was weak, and she did *not* want to show the extent of her weakness in front of Carter.

But he still noticed it. "You okay?" he asked her, frowning. "I'm sorry about Shelly. She's harmless, like, literally. I'll make sure that the guards know never to let her back in again."

She didn't exactly have a whole lot of faith in the guards. "I'm fine." Total and complete lie.

"Get some sleep," Carter said gruffly. "When you wake up, Griffin will be back."

He'd better be.

She didn't move, not until Carter had left the room. He shut the door after he exited, but that wasn't good enough for Isabella. Not when she kept having unexpected — and unwanted — company. She lurched across the room, then she grabbed the edge of a table that was near the door. Isabella shoved and shoved, and she got that table positioned right under the doorknob. Not much protection, but it would slow down any other *visitors* who might try to come her way while she slept.

Then, utterly spent, she turned back toward the bed. Every step was like trudging through quick sand. She was almost there. Almost...

She fell to the floor. Then Isabella decided — screw it. Sleeping on the floor would work for her.

***

His office had been torched. Griffin glared at the scene. Firefighters were still there, surveying the charred remains of the building. Cops were close by as they made notes and did their show of investigating.

And his office was gone. A blackened shell was all that remained.

Griffin inhaled, pulling in the scents of ash, water, sweat. *Fear.*

Humans were all around, gaping at the scene. On his way to the building, Griffin had wondered if Felix could be in the crowd, watching, waiting.

But the bastard wasn't there. Griffin paced closer to the building. The fire and ash were so strong they obliterated most scents. He had no doubt that Felix *had* been there — but the guy was gone now. *He stayed long enough to destroy my business.*

"What's next, alpha?" The question came from one of the werewolves Griffin had picked for his hunting team.

Griffin smiled at the wolf. "Now I make a call." Easy enough. He pulled his phone from his pocket and dialed the number that Felix had given him the first time that bastard had sauntered into his office.

Don't look into her eyes. If you do, she'll take your soul.

The phone was answered on the third ring. "Griffin?"

Yeah, that was Felix's pompous ass voice. And the guy had sounded surprised.

"I found Isabella," Griffin announced. He turned his back on the fire scene and stalked toward his waiting motorcycle. All of the wolves had come in on motorcycles. "Only you neglected to mention a few important facts about her to me."

Silence. Griffin let that silence stretch. He needed to keep the guy on the line —

"I didn't expect you to just...call me." Now Felix seemed confused.

Griffin laughed. Isabella would have told him it wasn't a real laugh. She would have been right. "We had a deal, didn't we? I was supposed to find the woman you thought was killing innocent men. I was supposed to get you proof of her guilt." He straddled his motorcycle, but didn't start the engine. "Only, it turns out…she wasn't the one killing." He waited a beat. "*You* were."

"Don't be so sure of that," Felix snapped. "After all, can you really trust a vampire?"

Yeah, I can. Tension had his muscles clenching. "I know about the other werewolves—the dead werewolves you left behind in your wake. And guess what, Felix? I'm on a new case now. I'm hunting again. Only this time, I'm hunting *you*."

"Ah…you found your torched office, didn't you?" Now Felix was pleased—and cocky. "Did that make you angry? I'm betting it did. I'm also betting that because of all the ash, you can't catch my scent from that place. The big, bad tracker…with nothing to go on."

Keep talking, asshole, just keep talking.

"You should be thanking me." The guy's taunt slid into Griffin's ear. "I introduced you to your *mate,* didn't I? I mean, you ran into that alley, and your whole life changed."

The guy wanted a *thank you?* Not happening. But Griffin would go with, "Fuck you."

"What I gave, I can take away," Felix threw right back. "Actually, I *will* take her away. Let's see just what that does to you. I've heard that once the bond is in place, if you separate the pair for too long, insanity follows."

What? Griffin hadn't heard that shit—

"At least, insanity for the werewolf. That's one of the many reasons why the wolves stopped mating with vampires. If you go too long without your mate's blood, without that sweet fix, you will plunge straight into madness. And won't that be something to see?"

Felix ended the call.

"Uh…alpha?" One of the young werewolves with Griffin questioned. "What are we—"

Griffin lifted his right hand. "Hold the fucking thought." Then he dialed again, quickly, his fingers too tight around the phone as he waited for this second call to be answered. *Pick up.* His contact picked up, and Griffin immediately said, "Tell me you got a lock on that bastard."

"Absolutely," Katie Fletcher told him. Sweet Katie—she was his contact at the Las Vegas PD. Katie had helped Griffin on more cases than he could count. Katie had a dozen grand-kids, a love for slot machines, and a very helpful job that allowed her to do a certain amount of side business for PIs in Vegas. Not that Katie's bosses knew about her side job…

"Triangulated the call, got pings from the cell towers nearby…I can tell you exactly where the guy was when you contacted him."

Griffin's hold tightened on his phone. Damn straight. He didn't need werewolf senses to track Felix. He had other methods. Had Felix forgotten Griffin was a freaking PI?

"Your target is heading out of the city, driving fast..." Katie rattled off coordinates, and when she did, Griffin felt his gut clench.

Oh, the hell, *no.*

***

"You look dead."

The voice drifted slowly through Isabella's consciousness.

"Do you feel this?"

And a sharp, white-hot pain pierced Isabella's chest. Her eyes flew open, and she screamed — or tried to scream — but the sound just emerged as a weak cry. It took her a moment to realize —

There was a knife in her chest.

Shelly smiled down at her. "So that's how you wake up a vampire. I'd always wondered."

She'd wondered...so Shelly had stabbed her?

"But you are weak, aren't you? Helpless." Shelly pulled out the knife. Blood poured from Isabella's chest. "I know what it's like to be helpless," Shelly added as her lips curled down.

You're gonna know what it's like to be dead. As soon as my strength is back...

Then Isabella heard thunder. Booming...

No, not thunder. Gunshots?

"Your mate should have stayed with you." Shelly shoved the knife into Isabella's chest once more. "Then we could have gotten you both at the same time."

More gunfire. Blasting.

Shelly heaved Isabella up into her arms, and then the redhead tossed Isabella over her shoulder. "I'm stronger than I look." She carried Isabella to the door. The table that Isabella had tried to use for protection was smashed into a hundred pieces. So much for that plan. "At least, I'm stronger now. It's because I've been getting some upgrades."

There were two werewolves in the hallway. Blood gushed from their chests.

"Silver bullets," Shelly explained. Her steps never slowed. "I walked right up to them and pulled the trigger. Dumbasses didn't know what hit them. Guess that will teach them to treat me like shit."

Isabella tried to peer around the hallway. Where was Carter? Where was—

More gunshots thundered. It sounded as if they were under attack.

"Felix is outside," Shelly told Isabella as the other woman carted her down the hallway. "It's gonna hurt you like a bitch when the sunlight hits, huh?"

What?

And then…then Shelly was opening another door. Isabella could hear the creaking of the hinges. Sunlight fell on them, and Isabella began to scream.

CHAPTER TEN

Something hit her — something big and strong and hard — and Isabella found herself tumbling out of Shelly's arms. Isabella flew through the air and landed back inside the mansion, on the marble floor of the foyer.

"You betrayed your own kind!"

Isabella glanced up. That was Carter screaming. Carter — he'd been the one to come barreling through the door. He'd knocked Isabella out of Shelly's hold, and he stood — bullet holes in his body — glaring at the redhead who was also sprawled on the floor.

Shelly rose, laughing. "My own kind?" She tossed back her hair. "Hardly."

Isabella sucked in a slow, deep breath. The sun had scorched her, but she was okay. *I need to be stronger.*

"My own kind treated me like *shit!*" Shelly screamed.

The gunfire had stopped. Carter was positioned a few feet away from the open door — Shelly was now right in front of it.

"You don't know," Shelly raged as spittle flew from her mouth. "You and Griffin, you weren't raised in this area. You don't know what my whole life was like. I wasn't a *real* werewolf, so they made my life hell. *Hell.* Did you think I was going to take that forever? Did you think I was going to be weak?"

There was a knife on the floor. The same knife that Shelly had used when she'd stabbed Isabella. Isabella crept toward it, every movement requiring maximum effort. Was that a silver blade? It looked as if it was...

"I'm not weak any longer." Shelly's voice seemed to echo around them. "I was always meant for more! Felix showed me that!" Then she bared her fangs — *fangs.* Fangs that looked just like a vampire's.

What. The. Hell?

"I'm strong..." Shelly lifted her claw-tipped fingers. "And you, Carter, you're just another dead werewolf."

She raced toward him. Isabella kicked out her feet, and she tripped Shelly. Shelly fell with a scream, and she was still screaming when Isabella lurched up and drove the silver knife into Shelly's heart.

That's what you get...for trying to burn a vamp with sunlight.

Boom!

The gunfire blast was far too close. And…Isabella looked up just as Carter fell, slamming down onto the tile right next to her.

Felix stood in the doorway, his face twisted with fury. "You killed Shelly?" And behind him… was that the same bastard Isabella had fed on in the alley? The bastard who'd tried to attack *her* right before her fateful meeting with Griffin?

Carter was jerking beside her, and blood pumped out of him. Isabella slapped a hand toward him. *Drink…* She couldn't manage to speak the command, but she sure hoped he could take a hint.

Luckily, he could. Isabella felt Carter grab her hand. And then she felt his bite. If he survived, would he be obsessed with vamp blood? She didn't know, and right then, she could only focus on keeping him alive.

Felix bent over Shelly. His hand wrapped around the knife, and he yanked it from her heart. Shelly didn't move.

"That's a fucking waste," Felix said with a long sigh. "After all the trouble we went to with her…and she was showing such promise! Her vampire traits were finally emerging! She'd been able to drink from the werewolves!"

The man with Felix— *definitely the asshole from the alley!* — had also bent at Shelly's side. "I liked her. She was fucking phenomenal in the sack."

"I liked her, too, Will," Felix muttered. "She was a rare find."

Carter let go of Isabella's hand. His body had slumped on the floor. Had he taken enough blood to heal? Or had the guy just passed out? "Carter..." Isabella whispered.

The guy called Will looked up. His gaze met hers. "I am going to hurt you so much," he promised. He surged toward her, but Felix shoved his hand on Will's chest.

"We need her." Felix turned his head and stared at Isabella. "*I* need her. She lives. You can hurt her, but she lives."

Oh, damn, but this *sucked.*

Felix turned his back on Shelly. He moved toward Isabella, the gun still cradled in his hand. "The weakness is the worst part, isn't it? I mean, here you are, with this incredible lifespan, this eternal youth, but during the day, you're a prisoner to your own body. *That's* the one part I hate. And I was so close to finding a cure."

Her eyelids wanted to close. She fought to keep them open. Sunlight spilled in through the open doorway, almost reaching her feet.

"The werewolves are the key, I know it. Take Shelly over there...she was primarily a werewolf, but when I looked back far enough in her family tree, I realized that her great-grandmother was a vamp. Shelly was a very, very rare breed. Werewolves and vamps aren't supposed to have children together, it shouldn't be possible with the different genetics, but it happened. *It happened.* And the vamp's power stayed in the bloodline. It was strong in Shelly, that's why she couldn't ever shift. Her vampire side was stronger than her wolf. I just needed to push her, to give her the right guidance, and then nature took over."

Nature? Looked like nature hadn't taken over that much...vamps didn't die when silver hit their hearts, but Shelly was *gone.*

"A bit more blood and her transformation would have been complete." Felix grabbed Isabella's arm and dragged her to her feet. "You screwed that up."

Good.

He put his mouth to her ear. "I'm going to kill your mate. It'll be payback."

Fear surged inside of her. *No, not Griffin!*

"I gave him to you, and now I'll take him away."

No, *no.*

"Carry her ass out, Will. We need to leave before the dead start stinking up the place."

***

The blood was still fresh when Griffin arrived back at the mansion. The guards who should have been patrolling outside of the place were dead, their bodies were filled with silver bullets, and their blood soaked the ground beneath them.

Griffin raced inside the mansion, bellowing for Isabella, but he only found more death.

Shelly was on the floor, a pool of blood surrounding her. A silver knife had been tossed at her side. And…there was a blood trail to her right. As if someone had been dragged down the hallway.

Griffin followed that trail. His claws were out, his beast snarling for freedom. He was so desperate to get to Isabella…

The blood trail led to the room she'd been inside. The same room where they'd made love. The same room—

Carter. Carter was slumped in the doorway, and the blood trail had come from him.

"She's…not here, man." Carter licked his lips. "Bastard…took her."

Griffin crouched at his side. Blood covered Carter's chest. Griffin reached for the guy—

"No." Carter shook his head. "I…already got the bullets out. I'm healing. Isabella…she offered her blood to me."

What?

"It gave me the strength to survive." Deep lines bracketed his mouth. "Shelly…she betrayed us. She was working with that Felix…that bastard the whole t-time…"

"Where did he take Isabella?"

"Don't know…but…h-he's going to h-hurt her…"

No, he fucking wouldn't. Felix was just going to *die.* Griffin slapped his hand on Carter's shoulder. "I'll bring her back." Then he stalked past the dead. He went back outside. Fury hardened his entire body.

"Are you...are you going to call him again, alpha?" The quiet question came from the young werewolf who stood near the front door. One of the guys who'd been hunting with Griffin in Vegas. "And...use that contact you had at the PD for another trace?"

"Don't need to." He rolled back his shoulders. "I can find my mate anywhere. Anytime." And he would. He'd go straight to her.

No matter where Felix had taken her, no matter how smart the bastard might think he was, Griffin would find Isabella. Her scent was in his very soul.

"And when I do find her..." A growl broke from him. "The humans will *die*."

***

The sun had set. Isabella could feel the night wrapping around her. A faint smile curved her lips as she opened her eyes and gazed at the man Felix had called Will. "You've made a very bad mistake."

He laughed at her. "No, we haven't. Felix doesn't make mistakes. While you were out cold, we flew your ass out of Nevada. It's been *hours*. Your werewolf won't find you. No one will find you. Felix can cut you open, he can run all of his tests, and you can just scream your head off.

Scream as loud as you want—no one will hear you."

She was in some kind of old, stone room, and heavy, metal chains were locked around her wrists. Those chains were attached to the stone behind her. *A cell.* Felix had obviously planned long and hard for this little end game of his.

He just hadn't counted on all of the variables.

Will stepped closer to her. An evil grin twisted his face. "Gonna try working a compulsion on me? Go ahead, give it your best shot. 'Cause it won't work." He pointed to his eyes. "I'm wearing special contacts that Felix gave me. He's so fucking smart. Way smarter than you. He figured out a way to block the power of your gaze. According to Felix, all you're doing is some hypnotic bullshit. With the contacts in—or the glasses that Felix wears—your tricks don't work on us."

You don't even know all of my tricks.

The guy inched closer. She could feel his breath blowing against her face.

"He's going to hurt you," Will promised with dark satisfaction. "He wants to live forever, but not have your weaknesses. A link between a vampire and a werewolf is the key—I've heard him say that over and over again. You'll be his key. He'll study your blood, your body, he'll use you in order to get at that werewolf mate you took and—"

She ripped the chains right out of the wall.

Will's mouth fell open in shock. He started to scream, but she was on him before he could make a sound. Her fangs tore into his throat and his blood poured into her mouth. She drank, taking the blood to give her power, and then when she was done...

Isabella broke his neck. He fell at her feet. She swiped a hand over her mouth. "Your mistake...and Felix's mistake. You don't *know* me. You don't know what I've done." She broke the chains that bound her wrists. They fell to the stone floor in pieces so that she was completely free. "And you don't know what I'll do to protect what is *mine*." The idiots had wasted their advantage. They hadn't killed her during the hours of sunlight.

Now she'd destroy them in the darkness.

Because you will not hurt my mate.

The bond was there, undeniable. Bright and strong inside of her. She wanted Griffin, and no one would take him away from her.

Felix and any humans on his side would find out just how dark she'd been during her early years. They were about to see how vicious a born vampire like her could truly be.

Isabella stepped over the dead man and walked out of her prison.

***

Snow covered the ground. To the right, a long, sprawling building seemed to sweep into the side of the mountain.

Isabella was in that building.

Griffin had tracked her scent to the small airport outside of Vegas, then he'd beaten the hell out of the bastard who'd been left behind at that place—another of Felix's goons. The human had been desperate to stop his pain, so he'd told Griffin *exactly* where Felix had gone.

Even without the human's help, Griffin would still have found Isabella. His body had felt physically pulled toward her. As if they were connected by some invisible string.

They would *always* be connected.

He'd gotten a plane and followed her. A plane full of his pack because he'd brought plenty of werewolves with him. The better to attack. Felix had his own army—at least ten men patrolled the outskirts of that building. Griffin's werewolves would take care of them. And *he* would get inside. He'd get Isabella.

They had a future waiting. A very long life. Nothing would come between them.

He nodded to the wolves, and they took their cue. Already shifted, the beasts sprang forward as howls ripped from their throats. The humans started firing, but the wolves easily dodged those bullets.

Not so easy when you're the one under attack, is it?

Griffin tore off his clothes and let his own beast out. The transformation was brutal and fast, and the wolf snarled his fury at the night. He bounded forward, his whole focus on the building — and the precious prize inside.

Isabella.

His Isabella.

CHAPTER ELEVEN

She didn't make a sound as she stalked her prey. Isabella crept down the hallway. Her target was close. He *had* to be close. Felix had gone to great lengths to get her, so she didn't think he'd just rushed away and left her now.

She turned the corner and crept into a lab. An exam table was in the middle of the room, surgical instruments were to the right, vials of blood to the left, and sitting there, curled over a microscope...Felix.

She smiled and stepped forward.

"So...Will is dead." Felix turned toward her. He was in one of those rolling desk chairs, and the wheels squeaked as he moved to face her. "I watched the attack on my video feed." He pointed toward a computer screen on his right. "You were absolutely vicious. Definitely lived up to your reputation."

She grabbed him by his neck and jerked him out of the chair. Did he think this was the part of the story where they talked? Where she learned his back story? Screw that. She didn't *care* about his back story.

Isabella snapped his neck. The snap was particularly satisfying to her. She let his body fall. He sprawled on the floor.

"You will never hurt Griffin."

Felix's eyes snapped open. "Don't be too sure of that."

What?

He grabbed her ankle and yanked, hard. She fell, and her head slammed into the stone floor. His laughter seemed to surround her. "Oh, Isabella," Felix sighed. "What on earth made you think I was human?"

She jumped back up, her hands flying toward him, but—Felix moved faster than she did. He grabbed a syringe, and he drove it into the side of her arm. As soon as the needle sank into her, she felt an icy cold shoot through her veins. Isabella shoved against him, and Felix let her go.

But the cold just got worse.

"I needed to experiment on you before I tried the cure on myself," Felix said.

Cure?

"I couldn't just try *any* ordinary vampire. That shit wouldn't work. I'm a born, after all, which makes me a rare breed. And then add in the fact that my body chemistry is so different because I mated a wolf five centuries ago…and, well, you can see why I had to pick *you*."

Mated a wolf. Mated a—

Isabella fell to the floor. The terrible cold was closing around her heart.

Felix positioned himself so that he was standing over her. "It's because you saw me in the day, right? That's why you thought I was human?" He knelt beside her and smoothed a lock of her hair out of her eyes. "That's one of the bonuses that comes from mating a werewolf. If you'd had the time, you would have seen that for yourself." He tilted his head to better study her. "Feed on their kind long enough—the way that you can only feed with a mate because the bond *has* to be there—and you'll start to get some of their powers, just as they get some of ours. After the first year, the sunlight didn't bother me. I could stay out all day and be at peak strength."

Her heartbeat was slowing.

"It was a good life, for a while." He still had the syringe in his hand. He glanced at it, then tossed it away. "Then my mate died. It's the werewolves who are supposed to get addicted, you know. They're the ones who are supposed to crave *us*."

She could barely breathe. Her hands clawed at the stones beneath her.

"But it's been one hundred years, and I still need her just as fucking much." Fury blasted in each word. He reached for his glasses and tossed those aside. "By the way, the compulsion didn't work on me because compulsions never work on other vampires...back at your hotel in Vegas, I just told you that bullshit about the glasses." He laughed. "And I told Will the bullshit about his contacts. The truth was…Will was already under *my* compulsion, so I knew any compulsion you tried to give wouldn't have a chance of working on him." His lips twisted. "Of course, you didn't go the compulsion route with him, did you? You just went straight for his death. Very bloodthirsty of you."

The cold was the worst in her heart, and, oddly, in her right wrist. *Where Griffin bit me.*

"I have to end the craving. The constant *ache* because Layela isn't here any longer." Felix shoved his fist over his heart. "I have to find the cure."

"Cure…" Isabella could barely force out the word. *And did I just hear a wolf howl?* "For…vampirism?"

He laughed again, even harder this time. As if she'd just told the most hilarious joke ever. "Oh, dear hell, no. I'd never want to be cured of that." He put his hand to her throat. "Your pulse is slowing down. I was worried about that…death might come, not the cure I want." Frustration hummed in his voice. "If that happens, I'll have to start all over again!"

"What cure?"

She heard a howl—she *definitely* heard it that time because the sound had come from very close by. Isabella managed to turn her head, and she saw a big, black wolf—a wolf with Griffin's green eyes—standing just a few feet away. He'd found her. She wanted to smile for him, but—

"The cure isn't for vampirism." Felix rose. And he pulled a gun from beneath his coat. "The cure is to end the mating bond. To sever it." He aimed the gun at the wolf. "Did you hear me, *Griffin?* I'm cutting the tie between you."

The wolf leapt forward. Felix fired. The bullet slammed into the wolf, but Griffin didn't stop. His claws hit Felix, and they crashed to the floor.

Felix fired again.

Isabella tried to crawl toward Felix and Griffin. She tried—

Blood. The scent is so strong. Blood and...silver?

"Liquid silver," Felix snapped. "How do you like that shit? I bet it *burns.*" He heaved the wolf off him. And, once more, Felix rose. Unstoppable freaking Felix. He still had the gun in his hand. His gaze darted to Isabella. "Still with me?"

She was going to *kill* him.

The wolf's body was slowly changing, sliding back into the form of a man as the fur seemed to melt from his body.

"In order to test the cure, I had to find another born vampire who mated with a werewolf. I had to get the mating bond in place...if I didn't have a vamp *with* the bond, then how could I break it?" Felix's words came faster now. "Couldn't experiment on me...what if the cure didn't work? I'd kill myself...and I don't want to die."

She crawled toward Griffin. He was so still.

"You're probably wondering what's in the cure..."

No. She was wondering how the hell she was going to kill Felix—and save Griffin.

"Silver is in it. Silver was a necessary ingredient because the mating bite *linked* you. Thanks to the bite, you have part of his beast inside of you, and I have to kill that part. I found a witch in Rome back in the 1950s. She was able to help me create some of the other ingredients. A mix of science and magic…a cure that could sever the bond by freezing the heart." He smiled, and it was a madman's smile. "If it works on you, then I'll finally, *finally* be able to live a damn day…" His shaking voice rose. "I'll live a day without feeling as if my Layela ripped out my soul when she died!"

Isabella touched Griffin's shoulder. "G-Griff…"

His head rolled toward her. His eyes seemed so dull. His skin was ashen.

"Griffin has quite a bit more silver in him than you do, my dear," Felix told her. "I'm afraid that's another part of the cure. The werewolf mate *has* to die, you see. As long as he lives, a part of you will feel drawn to him. To see if the cure truly works, you have to experience everything I did. You have to lose your mate. Only then can I know that the *gaping fucking hole* inside goes away with the cure."

Griffin was dying. Right in front of her. *No.* Isabella shoved her hand to his mouth.

But Felix grabbed her by the neck. He picked her up—as if she weighed nothing—and he tossed her across the room. Isabella hit the wall with a thud.

"No!" Felix bellowed. "No, no, no! You don't get to cheat! You don't get to heal him! Didn't you hear me? He has to die…and you have to feel his *loss!*"

The guy was a freaking psycho. Had he gone crazy when his mate died? Or just absolutely lost his sanity in all of the years he'd lived without her? Didn't matter. He was still going to die that night.

Felix stalked toward her. Isabella pushed herself up. And, behind Felix, she saw Griffin stagger upright. He was in the form of a man, but she caught the flash of his claws.

I have to distract Felix. He needs to focus only on me. "Do you want to know what the cure feels like?"

Felix hurried closer.

Griffin bled…and lurched after him, not making a sound.

"It's ice," Isabella whispered. She could barely stand. "It spread through my veins like the cold touch of death. Then it…centered…"

"Where?" Felix demanded, wide-eyed. Right. This was his grand experiment. He'd want all the details.

"M-my heart…" The heart that she couldn't even feel beating any longer. But it had to be beating, didn't it? Or else she wouldn't be alive. *Am I alive?* "And...my wrist..." Her shaking hand rose and she turned her wrist toward him.

"Is that where he bit you?" Felix's expression was frantic. "Is that—"

Griffin's claws sank into Felix's back. Felix screamed and tried to whirl toward Griffin, but Isabella was attacking, too. She grabbed the gun from Felix, and she fired at him, shooting him in the head, firing until the gun just clicked.

Felix fell, but Isabella couldn't move. Her whole body had gone numb, and, as if from a distance, she heard herself say, "He's a vamp...he'll come back...he's..."

Griffin's claws came down once more, and Felix lost his head.

"Not this time," Griffin rasped. "He won't...come back."

The surefire way to kill a vamp? Take the head.

She tried to smile at Griffin. They'd won. They'd defeated the bad guy. Everything was supposed to be all right now.

But then Griffin's knees hit the floor. He toppled forward, slamming into her, and they both fell. Griffin landed on top of her. *Liquid silver.* Those bullets had been full of liquid silver. She shoved against him, but her strength was gone, and he was so heavy that she couldn't move him. "Griffin?"

Her hands slid weakly over his shoulders. His skin wasn't warm. He was always warm—or he had been. But he was ice cold then.

He's dying. Normally, if a werewolf had been shot with a silver bullet, he'd just dig the bullet out. Or at least, she figured that was what he'd do. How did a werewolf handle liquid silver? *Could* he handle it?

"Griffin?" *I gave him my blood in the alley. When he was stabbed with a silver knife, my blood healed him.*

His mouth was near her shoulder. She couldn't feel the stir of his breath against her skin. She could hardly feel anything...but fear. Fear was a deep, gaping chasm inside of her. Griffin couldn't die. She wanted him in the world. She needed him there, no matter what the cost.

She managed to bring her wrist near her mouth. Isabella used her fangs to slice open the side of her wrist, then she shoved her desperate offering toward Griffin's lips. "Drink it."

It wasn't about some mating bond. This was about survival. *His* survival. Because he mattered to her—mattered more than anything.

At first, he didn't take her blood. Isabella thought it was too late. She'd lost—

His mouth closed over her wrist. He started to drink, and then she felt his bite, a quick flash of pain. Strange...she was surprised she'd even felt that pain. For a moment, the pain burned bright...

Then she didn't feel anything.

He was still drinking, but her eyes were closing. Her breathing was slowing down, the way it did right before she surrendered to her day sleep.

Had the sun rose? No, no, surely not. It wasn't time. But her body was heavy. The consuming lethargy weighed her down. Her eyes shut.

He kept drinking…

Good-bye, Griffin.

CHAPTER TWELVE

Sanity came slowly. A ferocious hunger had consumed him, a cold blackness had surrounded him, and Griffin had needed to fight his way back to reality.

Reality.

A blood-soaked room—or lab? A dead man to his right. And...Isabella.

Griffin lifted his head, and Isabella's arm fell back, falling limply to the stones beneath her. Her skin was stark-white, her eyes closed, and she was far too *still*. "Isabella?"

She didn't stir.

He leapt to his feet. Weakness didn't fill his limbs any longer. He'd been shaking when he attacked Felix. Griffin had used every ounce of his beast's power to complete that kill. The silver had poured through his veins, and Griffin had been sure he was dying...

Isabella saved me.

She'd given him her blood. He—he remembered her wrist pressing to his lips. He remembered her sweet taste.

Griffin scooped her into his arms and held her tight. She still didn't stir. *"Isabella?"*

Nothing.

What have I done? Had he taken too much from her? Had he *killed* his mate?

No, no. *"No!"* Griffin roared. His claws slashed open his forearm, and he put the blood before her mouth. She didn't take it, so he rubbed her throat, trying to force Isabella to swallow. Trying to force her to live. Because she had to live, for him.

He'd just found her. They'd only had days together. He wanted a lifetime—a dozen lifetimes. He wanted forever. He wanted *her*. Always. Only her.

But the blood just trickled from the side of her mouth. She wasn't swallowing it. She wasn't responding. She was terrifying him.

"Isabella?"

He tried again, needing her to have his blood. He'd taken too much, Griffin realized that—he must have taken far too much from his Isabella when he'd been injured. If he could just give her the blood back, she'd be okay. *If she'd just take the blood back.*

But even when he forced her to swallow, she didn't wake. She didn't stir.

She just…her body grew colder.

And the beast inside of Griffin went dead silent.

***

"A transfusion?" Carter's voice was quiet as he stood at Griffin's side. "That's not really the way vamps are supposed to take blood, is it?"

Griffin didn't look away from the bed or from Isabella. She was on that bed, her skin as white as the sheets beneath her. A nurse—a werewolf nurse—studied the blood as it slid into Isabella's veins.

"I thought vamps needed to *drink* blood," Carter murmured. "Not get, um, *infused*—"

"I'm giving her the blood any fucking way I can." Griffin had tried to make her drink. It hadn't worked. She'd swallowed some of his blood back at that hellish pit where Felix had died, but Isabella hadn't roused. So he'd rushed her back to a werewolf safe house. She'd been there for two days. Two fucking days. She had a pulse, a very weak one, but her eyes hadn't opened. Griffin had stayed at her side the entire time, but he kept thinking…*she's slipping away from me.*

"I read the files at Felix's place." Carter walked around the bed, moving to the other side. The tapping of his footsteps seemed too loud in the quiet room. "You know what he was doing, right?"

Had Isabella's fingers just moved a bit? Griffin wasn't sure, so he took her left hand in his. Her skin was so cold.

"Felix was a vamp, and his werewolf mate died a hundred years ago. He missed her," Carter added. "Shit, you should see his journals."

Griffin didn't want to see anything but Isabella.

"They are filled with insane rambles about the world being dark. Being *hell* without his Layela. Felix wrote that he could barely breathe without her. That she was in his head every day." Carter whistled. "I didn't realize the mating bond was so intense. I talked to a few werewolves, and some of them have lost their mates to death. Despite the terrible loss, they kept going. They told me it *hurt*, but they got past their grief. They didn't go…well, ass crazy. But maybe it's different when vamps and werewolves mate. The blood exchange, the different genetics, the —"

"If she dies, I don't know what I'll do." Get *over* her? Fuck, no, he couldn't. "I don't know what my beast will do." His fingers caressed her inner wrist. "He's silent now, because he's afraid. But there's danger in his fear. The fear cloaks rage, I feel it. If she dies…" Griffin forced himself to look up. "Stop me."

Carter blinked. "Stop you…from what, exactly?"

Griffin just stared at him. "The beast will take over." Because the man would break. "I love her." Quiet, ragged. "Already…I love her. She's *in* me, and I am in her."

Carter rocked back on his heels. "Not if Felix had his way, you're not."

Griffin looked back at Isabella.

"He wanted to sever the mating bond. To see if he could do it, the crazy asshole set out to create another bond like the one he'd had with his Layela. He needed a born vamp to form a mating bond with a werewolf. So he put Isabella in the path of werewolves. Those others—Felix had eyes on them. His guards. They saw that the first three werewolves were going for the kill as they closed in on Isabella. They had no hesitations—I read all this shit in his notes—so Felix had his men step in. They stopped the werewolves."

"And Felix took blood from them before they died." Werewolf blood was too powerful of a commodity to waste. "That's why the werewolves had puncture wounds on their necks."

"Felix put her in your path, just like he'd done with the others. But something different happened with you two. The link forged, and—bam. Felix had his experiment. And once he had you, he could finally try to break the link that had haunted him for so long." Carter gave a grim laugh. "He was afraid the cure wouldn't work. He didn't want to die, so he needed Isabella to take the cure first. If she severed her connection to you and survived, then he wrote that he was going to try the same damn thing on himself—"

"That's it." Griffin sat on the bed and pulled Isabella toward him. Her head sagged back weakly. "That's fucking it."

"Uh…Griffin?" Carter questioned uneasily. "Are you sure—"

Griffin motioned him away—Carter and the nurse. "Get out of here."

"Look, man, I want to help." Carter's voice was flat. "I know I made mistakes with you two, but she saved my ass. I want to help her. I want to bring her back to you."

"You can't. Only I can." Because it wasn't just the blood loss that was hurting Isabella. It was the fucking cure itself. He thought that cure was killing her. *She needs me to survive, just as I need her. I have to get through to her. I have to bring her back to me.*

If they'd lost the mating bond, then he just had to bring it back. He had to *bring her back.* How…how…how?

"Get the fuck out," Griffin growled.

"The…the blood will keep transfusing," the nurse said. "It's set to—"

Carter hustled her out.

Griffin gazed at Isabella. "I love you." He pressed his lips to hers. *Sleeping beauty, please wake the hell up.* "I love you." He called forth the beast that had gone silent inside of himself, willing the wolf to give his power to the mate who needed him so badly.

He eased her back against the headboard. Griffin breathed slowly and tried to *think*. Isabella was his mate. The other half of his soul. If the cure had severed their connection, if it was *killing* their bond, he had to stop it. *Because killing the bond kills her.* He brought her right wrist to his lips, and he remembered when he'd bit her in that alley. That moment seemed like it had happened a thousand years ago.

What I wouldn't give to spend a thousand years with you, Isabella. He lifted her wrist to his mouth, and Griffin bit her, right in the exact same spot he'd bit her that first time.

We have to bond again. Stronger than before. Our bond can save her…it fucking has to save her. And when Griffin bit her, the power of his beast was in that bite. The wolf's fierce strength, his determination, the magic of the beast—it all poured into her.

Her eyes stayed closed.

No, no. "I love you," he said again. "And I will love you forever." He brought his own wrist up. He eased open her mouth and her fangs scraped lightly over the skin. "You have to bite, Isabella. That's what's missing. *Your* bite. You need to bite me." He was rambling and begging. Desperate. "Please, I know you're weak. I know you're tired. But if you bite me, everything will be okay." Because he didn't think it was about the blood.

It was the *bite*. The one that wasn't supposed to happen anymore. Vampire and werewolf.

Taboo.

Forbidden...

Screw that.

"Nothing about us is forbidden. Do you hear me? We are *meant* to be. I was born to be yours, and you were born to be mine, sweetheart. So I need you to bite me. The power is in the bite. That poison cure he put in you? We're going to get rid of it. We're going to blow it straight to hell." He hoped. "I just need you to bite me. I need you to *fight* for me. For us. Live. *Bite*. Just—"

Her fangs sank into his wrist. A jolt of pure heat coursed through his body, seeming to bounce from him to her, then back again. Her body shuddered. He *felt* her inside of himself, touching his soul. The warmth and life that was Isabella.

His mate.

Her eyes opened. The color was weak, not so dark and warm, but her eyes were *open*.

Her tongue licked against his wrist, and her hand rose, hesitantly, to curl around his arm. Slowly, she pushed his arm down. Color began to fill her beautiful face once more. "Griffin?"

He kissed her. Hard. Deep. Desperately. Wildly. *Isabella. Isabella!* "You are never scaring me like that again," he vowed. He pulled her closer. Held her so tight, and let out a roar of absolute relief.

The door flew open, banging against the wall. "*Griffin!*" Carter yelled. "Is she—"

His roar hadn't been from grief. "My mate is back." And she would never, ever be hurt again. Not while he lived.

"Hell, yes!" Carter's footsteps retreated. "Hell, *yes!*" The door closed once more.

Isabella stared into Griffin's eyes. "I was cold."

She was breaking his heart.

"I couldn't feel you." Her fingers rose and pressed over Griffin's heart — the heart that beat for her. "I needed you."

"Sweetheart, I'll be with you forever."

A furrow appeared between her brows. "He was curing me…"

Griffin tensed.

Isabella shook her head. Her delicate jaw hardened. "No." Her voice was stronger. "He was killing me." The darkness of her gaze deepened. "You saved me."

"Isabella, you saved me from day one." He kissed her again. Relief was making him dizzy. Isabella — she was *okay*. The bond that his kind had feared — that bond had saved them both. "I love you."

She smiled for him. And his beast wasn't afraid any longer.

As he stared at her, Isabella appeared to become stronger, healthier. She ripped the IV out of her arm and shoved it aside, and then she was locking her arms around him. Pulling him close.

"They were wrong," Isabella whispered against his mouth.

"What?"

"All of the stories. The warnings. You didn't gobble me. You made me stronger." She licked his lower lip. "Griffin, I love you."

His breath heaved out. "And I live and die for you." Did she realize that? Did she understand—at all—just how much of his soul she owned?

Isabella gave a little laugh. "I think we're done with dying," she said, her voice a husky caress. "How about we try living—a very long time—with each other?"

To quote Carter… "Hell, yes."

Griffin kissed his vampire. Inside, his beast growled his pleasure. Then Griffin lifted his head and gazed into Isabella's beautiful eyes.

Don't look into her eyes. If you do, she'll take your soul.

She didn't have to take it. It had been hers from the very beginning, just as his heart was hers. And hers alone.

My Isabella.

Her mouth took his again, and, soon, Griffin knew he'd be taking *her.*

Forever.

The End

###

If you enjoyed FORBIDDEN BITE, be sure to check out BITE THE DUST by Cynthia Eden. Turn the page for a peek at BITE THE DUST.

BITE THE DUST
BLOOD AND MOONLIGHT
BOOK 1

Vampires. Werewolves. Beasts that hunt in the night. When New Orleans Detective Jane Hart investigates her first official homicide case, she never expects to have her world ripped apart. But the murder she's investigating is part of a deadly war between vampires and werewolves...and now Jane is caught in that eternal battle. A battle that can't end well.

Werewolf Aidan Locke has been running New Orleans for years. It's his job to keep the vamps out of the city. But when a Master Vampire comes to town, determined to unleash hell, Aidan knows it's time to fight with all the fury of his pack. Beast versus vamp, until the last breath. Then he meets Jane...

One look, one taste, and Aidan knows that Jane is far more than she seems. Far more than she even knows herself to be. She's important in the paranormal war, not a pawn to be used, but a queen to be won. And if he can't keep her at his side, if he can't stop the darkness from descending on the town...then Jane Hart will become not just a fierce cop, not some guardian, but something deadlier. Darker. Aidan will fight heaven and hell to change her fate. To change their fate because he is more than just a predator.

And Jane is more than prey. Far more.

The world is changing—for the humans and the monsters. Hot, sexy, and intense, BITE THE DUST is the first novel in New York Times and USA Today best-selling author Cynthia Eden's dark new "Blood and Moonlight" series.

BITE THE DUST
CHAPTER ONE

No one should die that way.

Detective Jane Hart stared at the broken body in the middle of Bourbon Street, a doll that had been cast aside. The victim's skin was too pale. Her eyes were wide open — dark — seeming to still show the girl's poor terror.

A crowd had gathered. Hardly a surprise. There was always a crowd on Bourbon Street. Jane could hear the whispers and rumbles behind her as everyone strained to get a look at the body.

The *naked* body. The victim had been dumped, just tossed aside, near the side of Hell's Gate. Music blasted from the interior of the bar, and plenty of folks were still packed inside the place.

How long had the victim been out there, those desperate eyes still open in death as she waited to be found? How many people had just walked past her before someone had actually stopped and realized…

She's dead. Not passed out. Not in some drunken stupor. She's dead.

The fact that her throat was ripped open—that should have given someone a freaking clue.

"Detective Hart?"

It was one of the uniforms, looking green. He'd been the first on scene, and when he'd called in the homicide, she'd been close by. Her captain had sent her over. *My first official case as a homicide detective.* More cops were coming—a crime scene team was on the way.

"There's so much blood," the uniform murmured. Mason. Mason Mitchell. A guy in his early twenties with light blond hair and the horrified gaze that told her he hadn't seen very many bodies before.

Maybe he was new to the beat.

There are always bodies in this city. Once upon a time, the Big Easy had boasted the highest murder rate of any U.S. city.

But things had changed.

Tell that to the girl on the ground.

"Just help me keep everyone back," Jane told him, rubbing at her right side. An old habit, one that she'd never been able to shake. Her fingers pressed hard in that spot, just for a moment, then she squared her shoulders. "I want a closer look at her."

Mason was right. There really was a whole lot of blood. Way too much for a typical scene. It looked as if the victim's throat had been slit wide open, from ear to ear. A horrible way to die but...

Maybe it was quick. The slice of a knife, then she fell.

The victim had been pretty. With long red hair and pale skin. Too young, far too young. But then, there were plenty of girls who were too young on Bourbon Street. They stood in dimly lit doorways, clad in negligees that offered little to the imagination, and they invited passers-by to come in for dances.

Jane crouched over the body, trying to be very, very careful not to touch the victim. The girl was on her back, with her hands spread out at her sides and her legs closed. Perfectly closed. *He posed her at death.*

Chill bumps rose on Jane's arms. The posing was *not* a good sign. *Right, like slitting her throat was a good thing.* Her eyes narrowed. There wasn't any strong light out there, and maybe that was why the girl had just laid there so long.

And not because the people just hadn't given a shit about her.

Jane pulled out her phone and turned on the flashlight app. She directed the light at the girl's neck.

No missing that horrible slice but...

Something else was there. On the left side. About a centimeter above the slice, Jane could see...

Two small holes. Puncture wounds? Yes, yes, they looked like puncture wounds.

Her gaze trailed back up to the victim's face. *No one deserves this death.* Jane wanted to take off her jacket and cover the young victim — *there was just something about her eyes* — but she knew that wasn't possible. She'd contaminate the scene, and the last thing she wanted to do was destroy any evidence.

She heard the cry of a siren behind her, and Jane jumped. She glanced back over her shoulder, her gaze cutting through the crowd, and that was when she saw —

Him.

Tall. Broad shoulders. He was wearing black — a black t-shirt and dark jeans. His hair was dark, too — dark and thick, as it framed his face. A face that wasn't handsome, but rather…dangerous. Intense.

Predatory?

Yes, the way he was staring at the scene was all wrong. The way he was staring at her was just *wrong,* and Jane's hand automatically went to her holster.

His gaze — she couldn't tell what color his eyes were — followed the movement, and a faint smile curved his lips.

What. In. The. Hell?

Her eyes narrowed as she marched toward him.

Other cops were finally at the scene. And she saw the flash of yellow police tape. Perfect. About time that area got sectioned off.

Two uniformed cops hurried toward her, blocking her before she could reach the guy who was *still* smiling.

"Detective Hart—"

"Secure the scene's perimeter," she said, getting straight to the point. "And get those idiots with the camera phones to stop taking their pictures." Yeah, she'd seen those fools, too. Frat boys who were laughing as they recorded. Drunk idiots. This wasn't some show—it was a person's life.

Death.

At her words, the tall, dark stranger glanced over at the frat boys. His smile vanished and she saw his square jaw harden.

Using his inattention to her advantage, Jane closed in on him. She saw his nostrils flare when she was about five feet away, and his head jerked back toward her. Their eyes met—for an instant—and then he backed away. Fast.

Oh, no, you don't.

She surged forward and her hand slapped down on his arm. "Excuse me, sir, but I'm gonna need a word." Her southern accent thickened a bit with those words.

Not a New Orleans accent, because that was a different beast. Mississippi. Gulf Coast. Because once upon a time, she'd been a Mississippi girl.

Until her world had ripped apart.

Her hand tightened on the guy's arm. He'd stopped backing away. Actually, he'd gone as still as a statue beneath her touch. A big statue. About six foot three, two hundred twenty pounds.

Maybe he was the kind of guy who used his size to intimidate people.

She wasn't intimidated.

"I'm Detective Jane Hart." She nodded. "And you are…"

For a moment, she didn't think he'd answer. Her left hand gripped his arm and her right was still poised just above her holster.

"Locke."

She waited, but there was nothing else. Jane let her brows climb. "That a first name or a last?"

His head tilted toward her. "She suffered."

He said it as if it weren't a question. Alarm bells were going off like crazy in Jane's head. The way this guy was acting—it was so *not* a typical bystander response. It was more the response of…

A predator.

A killer.

"Why are you out here tonight, Mr. Locke?" Jane pushed.

His gaze swept over her. She didn't like that. Didn't like him. He was making her feel too on edge, and where she touched him, her skin actually felt warm.

Bad.

Killers could be attractive. Alluring. She knew, she'd sure spent plenty of time studying them. Ted Bundy had certainly used his looks to lure in his victims. Handsome faces could hide horrible monsters, she knew that.

This guy isn't handsome. He's big and strong and dangerous.

"I own Hell."

Her hold tightened on him.

But he motioned to the club behind her. "Hell's Gate, it's mine. So when I heard about the body, I had to come outside. Terrible thing, this. Terrible."

He owned the club. The victim had just been left outside his place of business…right, not suspicious *at all*. "Did you know her?"

"I haven't gotten a good look at her yet."

She didn't believe those rumbling words.

"It's a shame," he suddenly said, his voice dropping, "what some people will do in this city…the lengths they will go to…people want to stay young and strong forever."

Jane looked back at the victim. *Dead far too young.*

"Good luck finding the killer," Locke said.

She turned her focus back to him. "I'll want to talk to your staff. They may have seen something—"

"They didn't."

He was too sure of that.

Her lips thinned. "Do you understand what cooperation is? Because if you don't, you're about to. When a woman's body is *dumped* outside your business, it's bad. Very bad. And when you stare out at the scene like you're some kind of — of — " Words failed her.

He waited.

"You look predatory," Jane said flatly as her hand slid away from him. "There is no sympathy on your face. You seem to be…" *Hunting.* But she didn't say that part, not out loud. She did have *some* restraint. Sometimes.

His head inclined toward her. "I hate this happened to that young woman." Now his words were coated with emotion — emotion that she actually wanted to believe. "It's a waste. A terrible shame. She should still be living her life and now things will just…end. They have to end."

Uh, yeah, about that…"I think they ended when some SOB sliced her throat open."

Mason called her name.

She didn't move.

"I have more questions for you," she said to Locke, a warning edge in her voice.

"I wish I had answers for you."

Okay, that was just a weird-ass response. She didn't have time for weird-ass anything. She glanced over at Mason. "I want you to make Locke comfortable in the back of a patrol car until I can question him again…"

Mason bounded forward. "Make who?"

"Locke." She glanced back at her suspect. "Make him—" Only he wasn't there. Locke had vanished, disappeared in an instant. "Sonofabitch." She surged forward, pushing through the crowd, elbowing her way past the frat jerks with their phones—still filming. Such assholes. *I will so be confiscating those phones later.* She didn't see Locke, not to the left, and not to the right. The guy had slipped away from her.

Jane whirled back to look at Hell's Gate. Did he really own the club? Or had that just been bull?

Mason rushed toward her, huffing. "The ME is here."

"Get in Hell," she told him curtly. "See if a man named Locke is there. If he is, drag his ass out for me."

"Um…do what, ma'am?"

"Drag his ass out," Jane snapped. Then she squared her shoulders. The body wouldn't stay out there much longer. The victim would need to be moved. And she wanted to be there. She wanted to make sure the ME saw those puncture wounds. Jane needed to make sure the victim was taken care of—the victim was her priority. And finding the girl's killer?

Oh, hell, yes, I'm on that, too.

She marched back toward the body. She'd be seeing Locke again. Very, very soon.

Her hand slid down to her right side. Pressed hard. The mark there, as always, seemed to burn...

***

Aidan Locke didn't usually hang out at police stations. But tonight was different. Tonight, there wasn't an option.

So he'd followed the pretty cop — *detective* — back across town. Mary Jane Hart. Though he learned that she didn't allow herself to be called Mary Jane. No, she was just Jane.

And, on the force, she was also all business.

Jane. Not exactly what he'd expected. Small, almost petite. A dancer's body and a warrior's mind. Such an interesting blend.

When he'd seen her earlier, her dark hair had been pulled back, making her eyes seem even bigger. Even darker. Her skin had been a warm gold. And her hand — it had been itching to grab her gun.

As if the gun would have done any good against him.

Meeting her had certainly been interesting. And the fact that she'd instantly looked at him and thought *killer* — well, that had been obvious enough.

And, unfortunately, she'd been dead on.

Before coming to the station, he'd made a little stop at the ME's office. He'd talked to the doctor. Made sure that the right stories were told. The right tests performed on the body that had been brought in to the morgue. He had everything covered. As usual. After all, it was his job to keep the dark secrets of the city hidden.

Someone had to be in charge of the place. And the humans — they just *thought* that they were running the show. No, he was the one pulling the strings. Had been for quite some time. And Aidan would be…for many, many years to come.

The current case was handled. The murdered woman would be forgotten. The matter filed away.

All that remained now was for him to have a talk with the pretty detective. He'd saved her for last. The shadows surrounded him as he waited for her to leave the building.

Someone sure liked working late…Another detail he filed away about the delectable Jane Hart.

All work and no play…

Well, it didn't make for a fun night in New Orleans.

Twenty more minutes passed, and then he saw her. She moved briskly down the police station's stone steps, and her gaze swept around the scene, as if looking for threats.

A threat was there, but she didn't see him. His prey never did.

She hurried down the sidewalk, her stride confident and quick, and he stepped out of those shadows to follow behind her. He didn't make a sound. Not even a rustle and—

Jane whirled toward him, her gun drawn and her body surging with a quick, fluid power. Before he could even blink, her gun was aimed at his heart.

"What kind of idiot stalks a homicide detective?" Jane snarled at him.

The woman had bite. He normally liked that, a lot. But this wasn't about pleasure. This was about business. Strictly business. "Stalking is a very strong word," Aidan murmured, "I was merely...hoping for a chat."

She didn't lower her gun. "So we could finish our conversation from earlier?"

He nodded.

"Conversation...interrogation...I guess you could call it whatever you wanted, *Aidan.*"

Ah, so she'd been digging into his life. He wasn't worried. The cops knew only what he allowed them to know. "Aidan Locke," he said, inclining his head toward her. "At your service."

The gun still wasn't lowering. So, he just stepped forward, and he kept advancing, until the gun pressed into his chest. "I didn't kill that poor girl."

"So your staff at Hell's Gate told me, again and again. The ME said the victim died less than an hour before she was found."

Made sense, considering that Aidan knew the killer would have only hunted at night.

"And everyone who works for you was quick to point out that you'd been having some kind of grand opening bash at that time, and you were right at the bar, serving drinks for all to see."

"Glad you checked out my alibi."

"I checked out *you*." Then, finally, she lowered the gun. But her delicate shoulders remained tense and her chin had notched into the air. "I also sent in one of the uniforms to find you right after that little disappearing act you performed on Bourbon Street, but you were nowhere to be found."

Light from a street lamp fell onto her face. A rather striking face. Not beautiful, but better. Her eyes were a bit exotic, turning up at the corners. Her nose was long, elegant. And her thick hair was slipping out of the ponytail and sliding around her face. Softening her.

Tempting him.

Not now. Business only. Pleasure later.

"I want to help," Aidan said. The words were true enough. He did want to help. He'd find justice for that poor victim. After all, giving her justice was his job.

"Glad to hear that." Jane nodded.

So serious. He knew quite a bit about the new detective. Facts that he'd read weeks ago when she'd first been vetted for the open homicide detective position. Though he doubted the woman realized *he'd* been the one to approve her promotion. When it came to homicide cops in the Big Easy, he always had final say. After all, he didn't want anyone getting in his way.

There was a status to maintain.

"If you're helping," she continued, "then I'd like you to turn over your bar's security footage from tonight. I could get a court order, but that would just take precious time. Time I don't need to waste."

No, he didn't imagine that she liked wasting time.

"I'll help," he said again, nodding.

"Good." She holstered her weapon. "And if we're going to talk, we're going to walk at the same time. I want to see what else the ME has for me."

The walk wouldn't be far. And the ME would have nothing for her. Aidan had seen to that.

But he fell into step beside her, automatically slowing his faster stride to match up with hers. Her scent wrapped around him—something soft. Feminine. Probably one of those lotions that human women were always using. He rather...liked her smell. What was it? He inhaled again.

Apples and...lavender. A nice blend.

Only...there was something more. A deeper, richer scent that was pulling at him. Drawing him closer to her.

Tempting.

"Are you sniffing me?"

He stopped.

"Because that is some weird serial killer shit if you're doing that. Don't make me go for my gun again."

From the corner of his eye, he saw that her hand was already near the holster.

"You smell good," he said, deciding to go with the truth. "But I'll try to stop the 'serial killer shit' for you."

"You'd better." Her steps didn't hurry. She wore boots and jeans. Jeans that hugged her legs and ass ever so well. He'd noticed the ass-hugging earlier, *before* she'd turned with her gun drawn. She had on a jacket, one that looked a bit battered, so he couldn't tell much about her upper body. He suspected her breasts were as perfect as her ass.

"I don't want lies from you."

Pity. He only had lies to give her.

"Did you know the victim?"

He shook his head.

"Her prints turned up in the system. She had a...solicitation charge against her. Melanie Wagner, age twenty-one. Just twenty-one. According to the intel I gathered, she was dancing at one of those dives on Bourbon Street." Disgust had entered her voice. "She didn't deserve to be tossed away like trash."

She hadn't been tossed away, though. He'd seen the body and had noticed the care that had been taken to position young Melanie just right.

"I will find her killer." It sounded as if Jane was making a vow. She should be careful doing that. It was never good to make a promise that you couldn't keep.

Up ahead, a small alley snaked away from the street. Darkness filled that alley, and, automatically, his gaze slid toward it. What a perfect hunting spot.

His tongue slid over the edge of his teeth. He could feel them starting to sharpen. "I certainly wish you luck with that endeavor." He started to say more, but then heard a faint rustle of sound. A light noise coming from the alley. Jane wouldn't have noticed it. Most humans wouldn't.

"Forget luck. Give me that security footage."

He stopped walking.

So did she.

Aidan forced a smile. "Of course. I'll call my manager right now and make sure the footage is sent to you." He pulled out his phone, but didn't call anyone. "I hope the ME has news that you can use."

Her gaze raked over him. "I don't get you."

No, she wouldn't. But she should hurry along to the ME's office. The streets weren't safe for her. Or rather, that *particular* street wasn't safe right then.

This problem shouldn't be happening. After he got the test results, the ME should have called in the clean-up team.

"No prior convictions, not so much as a traffic ticket," she said as she tilted her head. More tendrils of her hair escaped from her ponytail, and that scent of hers was seriously getting beneath his skin. "But when I look at you, I *see* you."

He tensed at that, wondering just what she meant.

"You're not some safe guy who plays by the rules. That's a lie. The image you're giving to the world is a lie."

She was hitting far too close to the truth. "So what am I?" *Who am I?*

"That's really what I'd like to know." She shook her head, sending those tendrils of hair sliding over her cheek. "Make that call. I'll be paying you a visit at Hell's Gate come morning."

Morning wasn't that far away.

Jane gave him a curt nod and then headed for the ME's office.

He called his manager and made sure his voice carried as he gave instructions for Graham to send the security footage to Detective Hart. And Aidan watched her walk away.

A truly great ass.

When she hurried up the steps that would take her into the building that housed the ME's office, his attention turned to the alley once more.

He could hear those rustles again. Louder.

And…a cry. A gurgle?

Hell.

The detective was safe, but someone else wasn't. He could smell the blood in the air. His hand reached into his coat, and his fingers curled around the wooden stake he'd hidden there.

Never leave home without a good stake. Advice he'd followed since his thirteenth birthday.

When he rushed into the alley, he saw the victim was struggling, kicking and scratching in the vampire's grip. And that vamp—the vamp was *guzzling* the guy's throat. A homeless man, by the looks of him. A fellow who'd made the mistake of thinking the alley was a safe place to sleep.

It wasn't safe.

"Let him go." Aidan's voice was sharp and hard. Cold with power.

The vamp ignored him. Kept drinking. The homeless man's struggles became weaker.

Shit.

"You're killing him."

The vampire looked up at him. Laughed. Madness burned in that gaze. Madness and power but the vampire *did* actually let go of the victim.

Then the vamp charged at Aidan, rushing forward with fangs bared.

Those fangs never touched him.

The stake drove into the vampire's chest, fast and hard and brutal. Straight to the heart. The vampire cried out and Aidan's arms wrapped around his prey. "It's all right now," Aidan said softly.

The vampire blinked up at him. Death was coming.

Aidan lowered the vamp to the ground. The alley was dirty. It smelled of urine and rotting food. The urine had probably come from the homeless man. During the attack he'd no doubt—

The vamp's hand grabbed tight to him. Like a claw.

Aidan could have broken away. He didn't. He stared down at his prey. When the life faded from the vamp's eyes, he was still crouched there, waiting.

After all, someone should stay until the end. No one deserved to die alone.

Want to continue reading?
Find BITE THE DUST at book retailers.

A NOTE FROM THE AUTHOR

Thank you so much for taking the time to read FORBIDDEN BITE. I hope that you enjoyed the story.

If you'd like to stay updated on my releases and sales, please join my newsletter list www.cynthiaeden.com/newsletter/. You can also check out my Facebook page www.facebook.com/cynthiaedenfanpage. I love to post giveaways over at Facebook!

Again, thank you for reading FORBIDDEN BITE.

Best,
Cynthia Eden
www.cynthiaeden.com

ABOUT THE AUTHOR

Cynthia Eden is a *New York Times*, *USA Today*, *Digital Book World*, and *IndieReader* best-seller.

Cynthia writes sexy tales of contemporary romance, romantic suspense, and paranormal romance. Since she began writing full-time in 2005, Cynthia has written over one hundred novels and novellas.

Cynthia lives along the Alabama Gulf Coast. She loves romance novels, horror movies, and chocolate.

For More Information

- *www.cynthiaeden.com*
- *http://www.facebook.com/cynthiaedenfanpage*
- *http://www.twitter.com/cynthiaeden*

HER OTHER WORKS

Wilde Ways

- Protecting Piper (Wilde Ways, Book 1)
- Guarding Gwen (Wilde Ways, Book 2)
- Before Ben (Wilde Ways, Book 3)
- The Heart You Break (Wilde Ways, Book 4)
- Fighting For Her (Wilde Ways, Book 5)
- Ghost Of A Chance (Wilde Ways, Book 6)

Dark Sins

- Don't Trust A Killer (Dark Sins, Book 1)
- Don't Love A Liar (Dark Sins, Book 2)

Lazarus Rising

- Never Let Go (Book One, Lazarus Rising)
- Keep Me Close (Book Two, Lazarus Rising)
- Stay With Me (Book Three, Lazarus Rising)
- Run To Me (Book Four, Lazarus Rising)

- Lie Close To Me (Book Five, Lazarus Rising)
- Hold On Tight (Book Six, Lazarus Rising)
- Lazarus Rising Volume One (Books 1 to 3)
- Lazarus Rising Volume Two (Books 4 to 6)

Dark Obsession Series

- Watch Me (Dark Obsession, Book 1)
- Want Me (Dark Obsession, Book 2)
- Need Me (Dark Obsession, Book 3)
- Beware Of Me (Dark Obsession, Book 4)
- Only For Me (Dark Obsession, Books 1 to 4)

Mine Series

- Mine To Take (Mine, Book 1)
- Mine To Keep (Mine, Book 2)
- Mine To Hold (Mine, Book 3)
- Mine To Crave (Mine, Book 4)
- Mine To Have (Mine, Book 5)
- Mine To Protect (Mine, Book 6)
- Mine Series Box Set Volume 1 (Mine, Books 1-3)
- Mine Series Box Set Volume 2 (Mine, Books 4-6)

Bad Things

- The Devil In Disguise (Bad Things, Book 1)
- On The Prowl (Bad Things, Book 2)
- Undead Or Alive (Bad Things, Book 3)
- Broken Angel (Bad Things, Book 4)
- Heart Of Stone (Bad Things, Book 5)
- Tempted By Fate (Bad Things, Book 6)
- Bad Things Volume One (Books 1 to 3)
- Bad Things Volume Two (Books 4 to 6)
- Bad Things Deluxe Box Set (Books 1 to 6)
- Wicked And Wild (Bad Things, Book 7)
- Saint Or Sinner (Bad Things, Book 8)

Bite Series

- Forbidden Bite (Bite Book 1)
- Mating Bite (Bite Book 2)

Blood and Moonlight Series

- Bite The Dust (Blood and Moonlight, Book 1)
- Better Off Undead (Blood and Moonlight, Book 2)
- Bitter Blood (Blood and Moonlight, Book 3)
- Blood and Moonlight (The Complete Series)

Purgatory Series

- The Wolf Within (Purgatory, Book 1)

- Marked By The Vampire (Purgatory, Book 2)
- Charming The Beast (Purgatory, Book 3)
- Deal with the Devil (Purgatory, Book 4)
- The Beasts Inside (Purgatory, Books 1 to 4)

Bound Series

- Bound By Blood (Bound Book 1)
- Bound In Darkness (Bound Book 2)
- Bound In Sin (Bound Book 3)
- Bound By The Night (Bound Book 4)
- Forever Bound (Bound, Books 1 to 4)
- Bound in Death (Bound Book 5)

Other Romantic Suspense

- One Hot Holiday
- Secret Admirer
- First Taste of Darkness
- Sinful Secrets
- Until Death
- Christmas With A Spy